# GHOSTS
## FROM THE
# JUNGLE

# RUSS STALLINGS
# GHOSTS
## FROM THE
# JUNGLE

*Ghosts From the Jungle*

Copyright © 2019 by Russ Stallings. All rights reserved.

No part of this publication may be reproduced, stored in a retrieval system or transmitted in any way by any means, electronic, mechanical, photocopy, recording or otherwise without the prior permission of the author except as provided by USA copyright law.

This novel is a work of fiction. Names, descriptions, entities, and incidents included in the story are products of the author's imagination. Any resemblance to actual persons, events, and entities is entirely coincidental.

The opinions expressed by the author are not necessarily those of URLink Print and Media.

1603 Capitol Ave., Suite 310 Cheyenne, Wyoming USA 82001
1-888-980-6523 | admin@urlinkpublishing.com

URLink Print and Media is committed to excellence in the publishing industry.

Book design copyright © 2019 by URLink Print and Media. All rights reserved.

Published in the United States of America
ISBN 978-1-64367-439-1 (Paperback)
ISBN 978-1-64367-438-4 (Digital)

10.05.19

# CHAPTER 1

*"We have let the warrior code rule our hearts
The death of a warrior does not mean victory"*

Erin Hunter (1967-?)

A slow rain falls as several ambulance jeeps pull into a hangar at Cam Rhan Bay Air Force Base, near Saigon, Viet Nam. The mood is quiet and subdued since these ambulances are bringing the coffins of those killed. Each coffin is treated with the utmost respect and honor. One final check of the identity of the bodies is made and then the coffin is sealed; a flag is then draped over it. The coffins are reloaded into the ambulances and transported out to the awaiting aircraft that will carry them on the first leg of their final trip home.

The occupants of the coffins are not aware of the pomp and ceremony that is being accorded them, those that are living and witness it, are moved by the solemnness of the display. Many of them think *'there by the grace of God go I'*. After the coffins are loaded onto the plane and it departs, another plane takes its place. This one for a happier trip but still equally difficult.

Once again, a parade of ambulances begins to arrive; but these go directly to the airplane and their cargo is unloaded directly onto the plane. These are the wounded that need more attention than can be given in a combat zone hospital.

These are the men who have had limbs blown off or other equally serious wounds.

In the distance, the faint booming of artillery can be heard but no one pays any attention to it; the sound is just a constant reminder of where they are. They all wish they were somewhere else, but this is the job they signed on to do and they do it to the best of their ability. As the men and women go about their jobs, another airliner arrives and is parked a short distance from the one being loaded with the wounded headed home. The soldiers on board the newly arrived plane watch silently as the wounded are loaded and once loaded the plane departs.

When the stair is finally in place the soldiers are finally allowed to de-plane, the officers are directed one way and the enlisted are directed another. The officers are loaded onto buses and the enlisted are loaded onto trucks. The distinction of the separation is subtle and very few pick up on it. The difference between the two groups was more than rank; there was also a disproportionate number of members of the lower income strata in the enlisted ranks.

The enlisted are taken to a replacement center where they will be assigned to whatever unit they were to spend their tour in Viet Nam with. After such a long flight, they were assigned to small compact tents that hold about twenty men. The men noticed an odor that permeates the air and when someone mentions it they are told that the whole country smells like that. They are also told that they'll get used to it.

They are granted the opportunity to grab some sleep and some food before they begin the next leg of their journey. Several hours after they lay down they are roused from sleep, formed up in the central plaza and given their assignments. One by one names are called and assignment orders are handed out. Soon there were less than twenty soldiers left;

the Sergeant in charge took down the names of the remaining men and said he would get back to them as soon as he could.

Kelly Broadwick slowly shook his head at the incoordination demonstrated by the army. He could not understand how such a large organization could not have a more streamlined and effective way to disseminate information.

"Broadwick!!" the sergeant called.

"Right here sergeant." Kelly called back raising his hand. The sergeant walked over and handed him a sheaf of papers. Kelly looked at them and asked what he was supposed to do now.

"Well…there is an "Air America" flight leaving for your base in about two hours from hanger three. I would suggest that you be on it." The sergeant replied as he walked away. Kelly just watched him go and then turned his attention back to the papers. The only thing that was different was the fact that the location of the base was blacked out. To Kelly this seemed strange, but he had been in the army long enough to know that everything would be explained when the time was right.

"Hey Kelly!" a voice called. He looked up to see Dick Van Meter walking towards him.

"Where did you come from Dick?" Kelly asked with a grin. Kelly and Dick had been in basic training together; where they had become friends. They had also gone through advanced infantry training together. From there Kelly had gone to jump school and jungle warfare school. Then to top it off he had been sent to sniper school where he finished at the top of his class. With Dick, he had been sent to officer candidate school and finished at the top of his class and as a result was given a commission as a first lieutenant.

"Actually, I'm here to collect your sorry carcass and drag it back to base." Dick said chuckling.

"Are you trying to tell me that I have to put up with you for the next year?" Kelly replied with a small laugh.

"Yeah, that's exactly what I'm telling you. If you haven't noticed there are silver bars on my collars." Dick said pushing up his collar to emphasize the point.

"Nice hardware…now tell me about what I'm going to be doing or is that a state secret." Kelly replied.

"I can't tell you exactly what you'll be doing but I can tell you that you were hand-picked for this assignment. Once we get to basecamp everything will be laid out for you. But, for now let it suffice to say that what you are going to be doing cannot be talked about…understand?" Dick said with a seriousness Kelly had never seen him use.

This struck Kelly as being strange because when they were in basic training and advanced infantry training, Dick was just one of the guys. He would joke with them and get just as drunk as any one of them. But now he seemed so serious, this would take some getting used to.

The two men continued to chat for a while then Dick suggested that they go get a cup of coffee. Kelly put his papers in his duffle bag and they walked over to the mess hall and got a cup of coffee and sat down at a table. This mess hall was different from most in the army because of the constant flow of soldiers they needed to stay open 24 hours a day and the others didn't. The two men used the free time to catch up on what had been happening to them since they parted ways after jump school. Soon Dick looked at his watch and said it was time for them to go. They headed back to where Kelly had left his duffle bag, gathered up his gear and headed towards hanger 3.

They got to hanger 3 and were told that their plane hadn't arrived yet but was expected at any time. Dick asked what they should do and was told to have a seat on the benches along the wall. Dick and Kelly made themselves comfortable on one of the benches and picked up their conversation where they had left off. Kelly asked questions about what he would be doing and about the living conditions.

Dick told him he couldn't tell him what he would be doing because of security reasons; but he could explain about the living arrangements. He explained that he would be living in a hooch with five other guys. They had a communal shower and a mess hall that served reasonably decent food.

"Hey Lieutenant, your plane just landed and will be here in a few minutes. As soon as they get re-fueled you can board." The sergeant behind the counter called to them.

Dick and Kelly watched as an Air Force C-130 pulled in front of the hanger. Shortly an Air Force deuce and a half pulled up to the plane and a man climbed up on the wing. He was handed a hose and he began the re-fueling process. While the re-fueling was going on several pallets of supplies were loaded into the rear of the plane. After about an hour they were told they could get on-board. Several other soldiers with rucksacks and M-16s started for the plane at the same time. One thing he noticed was that no one was wearing rank or unit insignias; Kelly made a mental note that he would have to ask Dick about this. After they had boarded the plane and found their seats, Kelly casually glanced at the faces around him. He absently wondered how many of them would survive their tour; how many would become a number on a report and then forgotten.

This is when it dawned on him that he was going to war. This wasn't a movie or any such thing…this was real. Now he was going to find out how much of those war movies he had seen was real. As the thought of the possibility of his own demise began to materialize in his mind he realized that he was in fact scared. Not the kind of fear that paralyzes a person with inaction, but rather the kind of fear that heightens a person's awareness of his surroundings.

"Hey Kelly...what's going through your mind?" Dick asked him after lightly slapping him on the arm. "This isn't the time to psych yourself out."

"Nothing...I was just thinking about home." Kelly replied.

"What are you worried about some girl? If she is really yours, she'll be waiting for you when you get back." Dick said knowingly.

"No not a girl...just thinking about how different this is from Texas." Kelly replied.

"Yeah...I would imagine this is quite a bit different from Texas; there they don't have little slant-eyed sons of bitches shooting at you." Dick said bitterly. The anger in Dick's voice surprised Kelly. He had never known Dick to be prejudice against anyone. But he supposed that was one of the causalities of war. One of the principles of psychological warfare was to get the soldier to dehumanize Kelly was shaken out of his reverie when the airplane began to shutter. The loadmaster moved towards the back of the plane telling all onboard that as soon as the plane landed they needed to get off as fast as they could. He didn't explain why but everyone knew that there had to be a good reason. They all began gathering their gear to facilitate a rapid exit.

The plane touched down hard, and the pilot immediately reversed the engines, they felt the force as the pilot made a hard-right hand turn and the loadmaster began to open the rear ramp. The plane hadn't been stopped two seconds when the loadmaster started yelling for them to move. When they reached the tarmac, Dick yelled for Kelly to follow him. They ran towards a bunker and were closely followed by the other soldiers and marines that were on the flight.

After they had reached the bunker, they crowded in and settled in to wait out the mortar attack. Kelly looked over at Dick with a worried look on his face; Dick just smiled and shook his head. This told Kelly that there was not a lot to worry about.

"Don't worry Kelly these walls are two and a half feet thick and they're only throwing sixty-millimeter mortars at us. This will be over in about ten or fifteen minutes or so." Dick said in a reassuring tone. Dick's comment made Kelly feel a bit better, but the explosions he heard still made him uneasy. When one hit kind of close Kelly ducked his head, this brought snickers from some of the more experienced soldiers.

"Is that you Van Meter?" a voice said from the dark shadows at the back of the bunker.

"Yes sir…it's me. I went down to the replacement center to get our package; but right now, he's a bit shook up." Dick chuckled.

"Good…when we leave here bring him over to my hooch. We'll brief him in and then you can get him settled in over in the first squad's hooch. But before you come to the office drop his stuff off. If Charlie starts his crap again I don't want to be tripping over a new meats stuff." The voice said.

"You got it sir." Dick replied. The conversation died, and they just waited for the thumping of the mortars to stop.

After about fifteen minutes of silence, Dick motioned for Kelly to follow him out of the bunker. When they got back into the bright sunlight Kelly took a moment to look around at the base. What he saw he was not prepared for, he saw orderly rows of canvas buildings with sandbag walls about half way up. Some of them had the flaps rolled up to permit the slight breeze to pass through. Here and there, in what passed for a street, he saw men with shovels filling in small craters, he assumed that they were where the mortars had hit. He smelt the stench of something burning but he couldn't identify what was burning.

"Hey Kelly, grab your stuff and let's head over to the company H.Q." Dick called to him. Then he Stuck his head back into the doorway of the bunker, "Hey Pete, is your jeep around back?"

"Yeah, are you going to barrow it?" a voice said.

"Yes sir, it's a bit of a hike over to first squad and I don't want to tire him out on his first day." Kelly said chuckling.

"Get out of here Van Meter." the voice called back.

Dick motioned for Kelly to pick up his gear and follow him. When they got to the jeep Dick told him to put his stuff in the back and to climb in. As Kelly started to climb into the jeep he noticed several bullet holes and a dark burgundy stain on the seat. He put two and two together and decided that it was probably blood. This and the mortar attack brought into sharp focus the fact that this was a real war not an exercise like in training.

He got into the jeep and they started off bumping and dodging around chuckholes. Finally, after about five minutes of a bone jarring ride they skidded to a halt in front of a canvas hut. Dick killed the engine and motioned for Kelly to follow him. Kelly grabbed his duffle bag put it on his shoulder and followed Dick into the hut. It was hot and smelled of wet canvas along one wall was several cots. Dick told him to put his stuff on the last one and they would sort out where he would sleep later.

They then headed back towards the jeep, but before they could get in and leave a voice stopped them. They turned in the direction of the voice and saw a gangly figure coming towards them. He was dressed in tiger stripe camouflage pants and an O.D. green t-shirt. His boots were all scuffed and unpolished.

"What are you doing up here in no man's land Dick?" the fellow asked. "Just letting the new guy put his duffle bag away before taking him over to Pete. By the way when did you get back? The last I heard you and team four were up at Pho Luc being used for target practice." Dick returned.

"Yeah...that one was a little bit hairy. We lost Alexander and Bobcat. Who's the new guy?" the soldier asked.

"Oh, I'm sorry...Denny Harwell, this is Kelly Broadwick." The two men shook hands. "Denny is squad leader of team four. He's also about the sorriest excuse for an officer I've seen lately." Dick teased.

"Yeah just as sorry as you are." Denny shot back with a smirk. Kelly couldn't understand how these two men could be so nonchalant about losing two of their men. Maybe after he's here awhile he'll better understand it.

The three men talked for a little while and then Dick excused himself and Kelly. They climbed back into the jeep and headed back to the main part of the base. As they drove Dick explained about him and Denny. Denny had been his training officer when he went through officer candidate school. So now Kelly understood their comradery. The conversation lagged which gave Kelly a chance to look at his surroundings.

The first thing that caught his attention was the contrast between the dark, drab green of the tents and the bright red of the soil. He was also struck by the large piles of spent artillery rounds. Off in the distance he could see low mountains that seemed to go on forever. Kelly's attention was snapped back to the business at hand by the nerve-grating sound of tires sliding on gravel as the jeep skidded to a halt at the back of a plywood and canvas building.

"Well let's go meet the boss," Dick said, "I think you'll like him. You two are a lot alike."

"You mean he's crazy too?" Kelly replied with a chuckle and a smirk. This brought a chuckle from Dick.

"Yeah...you're going to fit in here just fine." Dick said chuckling.

# CHAPTER 2

*Science may have found a cure for most evils, but it has Found no remedy for the worst of them all-The apathy of human beings.*

*Helen Keller
(1880-1968)*

Pete Philmore had been in the army for eighteen years and was thinking very seriously about retiring. He was beginning to think that being a commander was more for the younger men. The problem with retiring was that he was still quite young. What could he do if he retired? Would he have to take a menial job just to stay busy or would he be able to go through an employment service and find a real job? The pay at the job wasn't all that important since he would have his army retirement pay coming in. These were the thoughts running through his mind when he heard the knock on the door.

"Enter" he called. The door opened, and Dick and Kelly walked in. Pete had briefly seen Kelly but now that he could really get a good look at him he was struck by how physically fit he appeared to be. He guessed Kelly to stand about six foot three inches and tip the scales at about two forty. He was a very imposing figure.

"Sargent Broadwick reporting, sir." Kelly said as he saluted.

"Lesson one Broadwick, you're in a combat zone therefore you don't salute. That's an effective way to get someone killed." Pete said as he made a half assed salute. "Do you know why you're here?"

"No sir" Kelly barked standing at a rigid attention.

"Look Broadwick…lesson number two, we are an informal group here; there is no need for you to stand on military protocol unless there is a general here. I'm a full cornel and I set the rules for my outfit. Copy that?" Pete said.

"Yes sir, I copy that." Kelly replied as he relaxed.

"Alright then, take a seat." Pete said. "I'll give you the overview of what we do here. We do missions that the regular army is not equipped to do. We take out precise targets. Gather intel larger units would not be able to collect because of their size and in general not being seen doing it. Do you understand?"

"Yes sir, but with due respect, I don't understand why I was picked to join your outfit. I'm just a lowly Sargent, the rest of the people I've met here are officers." Kelly replied in a bit of a confused tone.

"Well…let me put it to you this way; if you can do the job you will get the rank. Ours is a very specialized unit… we're in the army but we don't take our direction from the army. We get our assignments from the Central Intelligence Agency. The spooks if you will. We are designated as a special operations group. That's why we don't wear any insignia or rank. I have been in this man's army for almost twenty years and this is the first time I have commanded a special ops group and I must say that it is fun." Pete said. "Do you have any questions so far?"

"No sir, I think I understand what you do but that doesn't answer the question of why me." Kelly replied.

"Kelly, you were picked because of your psych evaluation and the fact that you were first in your class at sniper school." Dick injected as he rummaged through Pete's refrigerator.

"In other words, I'm going to be a sniper in a unit that, as far as the army is concerned, doesn't exist. Is that about the size of it?" Kelly said contritely.

"Kelly, you have a good grasp of the situation." Pete chuckled, "Lesson number three is that we don't use rank when we address someone within our unit. So, my name is Pete Philmore." Kelly shook the offered hand. "Welcome aboard."

"Pete…you don't have any beer in the fridge!" Dick called, "What kind of bar are you running here?"

"The kind where that bunch of hooligans you're in charge of drank it all at the poker game last night." Pete chuckled, "Now get out of my damn fridge."

"I guess that means it's time for a class six run." Dick replied as he shut the door on the fridge. "That must have been one hell of a game last night; who won?"

"Yes, it was, and Stewart cleaned me out. Do me a favor Dick, tell Bill I need him to put another case in the fridge. Now getting back to business, Kelly I'm going to assign you to Dicks team, team two, for a while until you get the lay of the land. I have found that when you bring someone new onboard and you put them with someone they know, they tend to get into the swing of things a lot quicker." Pete said. Dick gave him a thumbs up and started for the door.

"Where do you think you're going Dick? We're not finished here yet." Pete growled as Dick pulled up short. "I have a mission for you and your team."

After Dick had regained his seat, Pete pulled out a map board and proceeded to lay out the operation to him. There were several back and forth questions about the reliability of the intel. Pete assured him that the source was reliable.

The basics of the operation was that they would be inserted about ten miles west of the village of Pho Luc. They would then move twenty-five klicks northwest and look for an enemy base camp. They were to determine the strength of the force and if possible take out the command structure. As the briefing was coming to an end Pete handed Kelly a piece of paper with the instructions to memorize it and leave it behind when they left.

When Dick and Kelly got outside, Kelly opened the paper and seemed confused by the broad horizontal red lines and the vertical gold lines across them.

"What is this?" Kelly asked pointing to the stripes.

"That is how the North Vietnamese designate the officer ranks." Dick explained.

"Why should I memorize this? It's not like I'm going to meet one in the field." Kelly said. Dick started laughing. "What are you laughing about?"

"Kelly...this is how you determine who your target is, by his rank. See the narrow stripes are junior grade officers and the broad stripes are the field grade officers. If we see one with a star he is an automatic target because that means he's a cornel or above. Understand?" Dick explained. Kelly stood and scratched his head.

"I don't know...this is all very confusing. Give me a little time and I'll get it." Kelly replied. Dick chuckled and patted him on the shoulder.

"Once you see the real thing you'll understand it very quickly. Come on, let's go over to the armory and get your guns then we'll go to the range and you can zero in. Once we get you set with weapons, we'll go over to supply and get your field gear." Dick said. Kelly slowly nodded his head in understanding.

When they got over to the armory, Kelly was given the choice of several rifles for his job. He was issued a standard

M-16A2 for field use. He then chose a bolt action 308 Enfield with a 500-power scope. This would give him an effective range of about half a mile.

After getting his weapons zeroed in and receiving his field gear they went back to the team four hooch to retrieve Kelly's duffle bag. As they approached the hooch they saw four men around the entrance and one of them was sitting on Kelly's duffle bag.

"Does this piece of trash belong to your newbie?" the man sitting on duffle bag challenged as they pulled to a stop.

"Yes, it does, and I would appreciate very much if you would get your fat ass off it." Kelly replied as he stiffened up preparing for the encounter he was sure was coming. This was greeted by hoots of laughter.

"OK, Lancer...we have established it belongs to him. Now what is the problem?" Dick injected.

"Just stay out of this Van Meter, I just don't like people coming in and dumping their crap on my bunk. Particularly a newbie." Lancer snorted.

"Look pal...I was told to put my bag on one of the bunks until after I got my assignment from the C.O. If you have a problem with that, then you need to take it up with Pete." Kelly spit back. This brought a smile to Lancer's lips.

"Newbie...you have just passed your first test." Lancer said, "You didn't back down when confronted. You're going to be alright, now come and get your crap."

As Kelly started to pick up the duffle bag Lancer grabbed him by the wrist, "Newbie, for the inconvenience of moving your bag outside you're buying the beer tonight."

"Says who, you make more money than I do; you ought to pay just out of the kindness of your heart." Kelly said grinning, "And quit calling me newbie; my name is Kelly Broadwick."

"Well Kelly Broadwick, I'm Jerry Lancer, the tall guy with the headband is Jim Tatum and the skinny runt in the corner is Robert St. Pierre, he's from New Orleans and I have to give him credit, he's a damn fine cook. He can do things with c-rats that will blow your mind. We're what's left of team four. We just got back from a mission to Tien Luc, as you can see things got a little dicey. We lost two guys." Lancer replied his voice faltering.

"What did you guy's walk into?" Dick asked.

"They dropped us about five klicks out and as we approached the village we smelled something that didn't smell right. When we got to the edge of the main compound we saw bodies laying all over the place; there were men, women and kids, they had been slaughtered; not just shot but cut up too. When we started to move towards the main gate they opened up on us from inside the compound and we beat feet for the trees. That's when we lost Bobcat, he took one in the back of the head. After we got into the bushes Alexander tried to return fire and got cut down by what sounded like an SKS.

We backed off and called in air support, they leveled the village and we moved back in. We counted thirty-two villagers and nineteen V.C. dead. We checked the bodies for papers but didn't find anything that would have helped us. Denny then called for a chopper and we got the hell out of there." Lancer dispassionately related.

That does sound like a rough one. Any idea which V.C. group was behind it?" Dick asked.

"Up there, it can only be one guy; Major Tau. He's the most bloodthirsty bastard I've ever heard of. He uses crap like this to scare the rest of the villages in the area onto compliance with his wishes." Lancer replied with a tone of disgust.

All through the discussion of the mission Kelly had been quiet. He had been listening to what was being said. With the description of the slaughtered villagers, Kelly couldn't believe that there were people that were so demented. How could someone kill an innocent child for no reason? This didn't make any sense to him at all. What bothered him even more was that these men could discuss it as if they were discussing a baseball game. He just could not understand how these men could talk about such carnage with so much dispassion.

The more he listened the angrier he became. But he wasn't sure if he was angry about the killing of innocent villagers or if he was angry about these men he was about to start work with showing no emotion over the deaths. Now he was about to become one of them; would he become just like them and lose all emotion towards the death of another human being or would he be able to keep his caring persona intact.

Kelly had been trained as a sniper and had come out of school at the top of his class. That meant that he was a killer; but he didn't see it that way. He was taught that all's fair in love and war. To Kelly this meant that if he went after only military targets then he was only killing the enemy. To Kelly what Major Tran had done to that village was nothing short of the same thing the Germans did to the Jews during world war two. He shared the disgust that the other men had displayed.

"Who is this Major Tau guy?" Kelly asked, "Is he some kind of warlord or something?"

"No…not exactly…he's more like a mafia boss. We have been trying to catch or kill him for about two years now; but he always manages to stay one step ahead of us. We're beginning to think that he has a spy inside the compound that lets him know about our operations." Lancer explained, "With this being a joint base with the South Vietnamese army, we can't just kick all the natives off the compound."

"I can see where that is a problem. But what if we could set up a fake operation that only certain civilians would know about. If the operation went off without a hitch, then we try it again until we find the right group. Then we could narrow down the list of people whom we would suspect." Kelly said. The men all just looked at him.

"That idea is all well and good except that we don't know where to start." Dick said.

"Well…where do you guys talk about your missions the most? In your hoochs, right? So, let's start with the hooch maids." Kelly said. The men looked at Kelly and then at Dick thoughtfully.

"You know what, that might just work. Lancer…where's Denny, I want to fill him in on this before I take it to Pete." Dick said.

"I think he said he was going to the showers." Lancer replied.

"Well, this isn't that important. I'll talk to him later about it." Dick said, "Kelly…Grab your stuff and let's get out of here." Kelly picked up his duffle bag and put it in the back of the jeep. Then he climbed in and waited for Dick.

After a few more words with Lancer, Dick got in the jeep and they headed off to the team two area. Though it was a very short distance away Dick drove a roundabout route pointing out various points of importance. The major one he pointed out was the mess hall, this is where they would be taking their meals whenever they were in basecamp. Dick also pointed out where the group club was. Then pulled up in front of team two's hooch. Dick told him to grab his gear and come inside. At first Kelly struggled to try to pick it all up and only make one trip, but when he tried to pick up his duffle bag it became quite clear to him that he was going to have to make another trip.

Kelly paused in the doorway momentarily to allow his eyes to adjust to the dimmer light, then walked over to a bunk that had the mattress rolled up.

"This Ok?' Kelly asked.

"No, that's my bunk. Take the one over in the corner. Jackson went home last week." Dick replied. Kelly unrolled the mattress and put his rucksack and rifles on the bed. This gave him a chance to look around the hooch. He noticed the picture of the girl tacked to the wall above the bunk Dick said was his.

"who's the girl?" Kelly asked.

"That's my girlfriend, Elizabeth. She's pre-law at University of Pennsylvania," Dick replied, "You got a girl?"

"Yeah, her names Doris and her father runs a garage in town." Kelly said with pride. The conversation was cut short when four men came noisily into the hooch, they looked at Dick and then at Kelly.

"Who are you?" challenged the first man in the door. The other three men looked on suspiciously.

"It's ok guy's...Kelly's our new man." Dick replied before Kelly could speak.

"This is Jackson's replacement? Is this guy any good or are we going to have to train him?" the second man through the door asked.

"Well...he graduated first in his class at sniper school and he's just as tough as any one of you...so my advice to you, is don't try him." Dick replied.

"Dick, you sound like you might have made that mistake." The first man said snickering.

"I'm not saying whether I have or haven't...but I do know Kelly and he's good. Just as good as Jackson was, if not better. I requested him for our team." Dick stated.

"OK top, we can take a hint. I'm Sam Holmes, they call me bumper." The first man said turning away from

Dick and extending a hand toward Kelly. The two other men introduced themselves as John Alcorn A.K.A. Slick and Dennis Mansger A.K.A. Manse.

"I've got the three stooges here, so where's Scuzzy Bill?" Dick asked.

"He went over to the motor pool something about someone owed him some money." Bumper replied. Dick just shook his head

"One of these days that man's going to learn to play cards with people who have money and can cover their bets." Dick said.

Just then a very muscular man came through the door. He was wearing a sweat stained t-shirt and a beat up boonie hat. His boots were scuffed to the point that there wasn't any black left on them except for the soles. The lower pockets of his jungle fatigues were so crammed with stuff that they seemed to be alive.

"Bill, where have you been? We're getting ready to have a mission briefing." Dick said sounding a bit miffed.

Kelly sat quietly on his bunk and listened to the banter of his new friends. They seemed to know each other so well that they sounded more like siblings then co-workers. But later, when they get to know him better they'll be having the same kind of loose conversations with him, but for the time being he felt very left out. Maybe he was homesick for his friends; with them he never felt left out. He was sure he missed Doris and his parents.

"Hey Kelly…you want to join us over here, so I don't have to repeat myself. This is important stuff that you're going to need to know." Dick said with a touch of exasperation in his voice.

Kelly got up and took the only remaining chair at the table at the other end of the hooch. After he was seated Dick began to outline the mission. He passed around photos of the intended target, Major Tau. He was the area commander for the North Vietnamese troops. They had been trying to either capture him or kill him for almost three months; but every time they got close he would slip across the border into Laos where they couldn't go.

The lift off time for the operation was set for two days away at day break. In the meantime, they had to get all their weapons ready and draw seven days rations from supply. Dick gave them all a map with orders not to mark on them. Kelly was beginning to think that this was going to be a walk in the park.

He was in no way prepared for the suddenness of the attack; one second, they were discussing the mission the next second all hell broke loose. Chair parts, dirt, dust, and bodies went flying in every direction. From outside he could hear men screaming in pain and others barking orders. Kelly was stunned and didn't know what to do until someone grabbed him by the arm and started dragging him towards the door. When they got outside he was pushed to his right and someone yelled for him to get to the bunker. He snapped his head back and forth trying to locate the bunker when something exploded at the end of the row of tents that sent several bodies flying.

Finally, he located the bunker and began to run in that direction; suddenly something picked him up and slammed him to the ground. For what seemed like a long time, that was mere seconds. he couldn't move. Then the next thing he knew two people grabbed him under the arms and started dragging him towards the bunker. As they dragged him he could hear several explosions close by. Kelly could feel no pain, but he knew he had been hurt; how bad he wasn't sure.

What scared him the most was the thought of losing a leg or an arm; but since these two men could drag him he was sure he still had both of his arms. The fear he felt was unlike anything he had ever experienced. It was a petrifying fear that invaded the very core of his being. *"But why don't I feel any pain? Am I already dead? Why won't my legs work?"* Kelly thought. Then he felt someone lightly smacking his face.

"Kelly...Kelly...can you hear me? Kelly are you alright?" a voice yelled at him. He couldn't make out the face in the darkness of the bunker. When he tried to roll over off his stomach the most intense pain he had ever felt shot up his back and he screamed in pain. "Just lie still we've got the medics on the way"

Moments later he felt hands grabbing his clothing and pick him up. Once they had him up a litter was pushed under him and he lowered back down on it. Once again, the pain in his back came to life but it was so intense that he could only moan. Two men quickly picked up the litter and hustled him to a jeep where they put the litter crossways. The short ride to the aid station was wracked with pain for Kelly. Somewhere along the way he passed out.

When he woke up he was in a cot he and in a building, he had never seen. On either side of him were other wounded men, he couldn't tell if they were sleeping or dead. Kelly was lying on his stomach and tried to roll over; again, the pain shot up his back, only not as intense as before.

"Well you finally woke up. How are you feeling?" a male voice said from behind him.

"I hurt like a son of a bitch. What the hell happened?" Kelly asked.

"You had a mortar land right behind you. You had a bunch of shrapnel in your back and buttocks. We took it out and put it in a jar for you. Do you think you can get up with a little help?" the voice asked.

"Yeah, I think I can. Who are you?" Kelly asked.

"I'm Nick Cummins, I'm the nurse on this ward. I'll go get a couple of interns and we'll get you up." Nick said.

He left and returned a few minutes later with two other men dressed in green T-shirts and jungle fatigue pants. He then explained how they were going to lift him into a sitting position then help him stand.

With a lot of groaning and some cussing, Kelly was brought to a sitting position. After a short rest and the help of the two interns, he was able to stand. He tried to take a step, if it hadn't been for the two interns he would have crashed to the floor. They eased him back down on his bed.

"Please tell me this doesn't mean I'm going to be a cripple." Kelly asked in a scared tone.

"No that isn't what it means at all. The damage to your legs is causing the nerves to react. In a few days you'll be walking just as good as before." Nick told him. Kelly looked at him with doubt written all over his face.

"Kelly, you don't have permission to become a cripple." Said a voice from behind him. Kelly painfully turned to see Dick standing by the door.

"How long have you been standing there?" Kelly asked.

"Long enough to see you try to plop your ass in the floor." Dick replied with his arms folded across his chest, "You have been here two days and already you've managed to get yourself messed up. I just wanted to see how good a job you did."

"Well…it's not by choice that I'm here. I really don't know what happened; I was running and then suddenly the ground jumped up and kicked me in the face." Kelly explained.

"You're going to be fine in a little while. You'll be sent back to the company in a day or two to rest up and heal. Then we'll get on with our part of the war." Dick stated.

"Yeah, you're going to be ok in a few weeks." Nick chimed in, "It'll probably take you a couple of weeks to heal but after that there shouldn't be any residual pain or bleeding."

"How long is it going to take for me to heal?" Kelly asked.

"That depends on you. If you keep everything clean, you should be able to go back to duty in about three weeks." Nick explained, "The important thing is controlling infections. You can help with that by making sure your bandages are changed daily for about the first week." Kelly nodded his understanding.

# CHAPTER 3

*Pain makes men think. Thought makes men wise Wisdom makes life endurable.*

John Patrick
(1905-1995)

As the days passed and Kelly became less sore each day. Soon he felt ready to go back to duty, but Pete wouldn't let him. In the preceding weeks Kelly had watched his team go out on several observation missions. He had tried to put on his rucksack, but his back had not healed enough, and the pain almost brought him to his knees. The pain he felt in his lower back wasn't from being weak it was from actual injury that hadn't completely healed.

In September of 1967, Kelly was trying his best to heal as quickly as possible so that he could rejoin his team and do his part. It seemed that the more he tried the less he was healing. Every day he would try to put on his rucksack and everyday it would hurt almost more than he could stand. But he did notice that each day the pain lessened just the tiniest bit. When he was finally able to put on his rucksack without his knees buckling a month had passed.

Finally, two weeks into October, he could put it on without pain. He reported this to Pete, who seemed to be pleased.

"It's about time…I'm getting tired of having you haunting the company area and bothering people." Pete had said with a grin. He then went on to tell Kelly that he was glad that he was finally able to get back in the action. Pete explained that there was a mission coming up that required his specific skills as a marksman. Kelly pressed Pete for more details, but Pete refused saying that he didn't want to have to repeat himself. Suddenly Bill Dunn, the company clerk came rushing in.

"Pete, we have a problem…team three just got hit and hit hard. Three are down and they're taking heavy small arms fire." He stated gravely.

"Where are they?" Pete asked.

"South and west of Phan Loy Duc, over on the border." Bill replied. "Has H.q. started anyone towards them yet?" Pete asked.

"From what Benny said 'C' company 3rd of the 2nd is in route as we speak. The gunships are on site and trying to give cover for extraction." Bill explained.

"OK…keep me up to date on it. When you find out about who's hurt let me know. I want a debrief as soon as they get back. I want to find out what went wrong; they were only supposed to observe." Pete said as he looked between Bill and Kelly.

Kelly just watched Pete and Bill in an attempt to figure out what was going to happen now. Would this effect the mission that Pete had eluded to? These were all questions that would have to wait until the mission briefing.

"Bill…would you get S-2 on the horn for me. I want to speak to Major Collins. Kelly you'll have to excuse me, but I need to take this call in private." Pete said apologetically. Kelly shook his head knowingly and him and Bill left the room. Bill went to his desk and made the call as Kelly went out the door and headed back to the team tent.

When he got to the tent, Kelly found some mail on his bunk. This was the first time he had gotten any mail and it felt good. After what he had gone through getting mail was a welcome boost to his morale. From the addresses he could see that he had received letters from his family and his girlfriend Doris. This was the letter he was most interested in, since he hadn't heard from her in almost two months.

Kelly and Doris had been quite an item back in Plano, Texas. They had been high school sweethearts and were going to get married; but then he got his draft notice and had to go into the army. An image of Doris formed in his mind as he reads her letter. She was such a sweet girl, she had lived on the farm next to theirs and they had known each other since junior high school. She had been the first girl he had ever kissed. The memory of that night started to play over in his head. He remembered how fresh she looked when he picked her up to go to the dance down at the Grange Hall. When they got to the hall Kelly parked in the back of the lot. Doris gave him a quizzical look and he reached over and gave her a quick peck.

"Kelly Broadwick…if you're going to kiss me you better do it right." She said in a huff, "I'm not the type of girl that will settle for no foolishness like that." So, he decided to scoot closer, pulled her to him and kissed her slowly and much more passionately.

"That's more like it." She breathed when he released her. Then she began to kiss him passionately and Kelly could feel himself being swept up into a current that he was totally unfamiliar with.

"Do you have a blanket in your truck?" Doris whispered in his ear. Kelly was so shook up all he could do was nod. "Good…let's go over to Lake Bailey." Without thinking, Kelly scooted back over into the driver's seat and started the truck.

Won't your folks miss us at the dance?" Kelly asked.

"They might but being alone with you will be a lot more fun." She giggled. As they pulled out of the parking lot Doris scooted over close to Kelly and began to lightly rub his leg. The drive over to the lake was only about fifteen minutes, but the constant contact only heightened his awareness of her femininity. With each rub her hand came closer to his manhood, this told him exactly what she had on her mind.

When they got to the lake he started to pull into the parking lot, but Doris directed him to pull around to the other side of the lake. She told him that it would be quieter there and they wouldn't be disturbed. Kelly followed Doris' directions around the lake to a very secluded spot by the falls that fed the lake. When they finally stopped Doris jumped out and started running towards the water, as she went she took off her clothes. This was not only a surprise but a shock to Kelly. He had never seen a real girl naked.

When she reached the water's edge she turned back towards Kelly and called for him to come on. Kelly was dumbstruck at the sight of her in the moonlight. The whiteness of her body seemed to glow and shimmer. The swell of her breast was as surprising as anything he had ever seen. The way they shifted from side to side when she moved fascinated him to a point that he couldn't take his eyes off them. Her nipples and areolas looked like targets on her chest. Farther down below her flat and seemingly muscular stomach, the growth of her pubic seemed out of place with the whiteness of the rest of her body.

Suddenly as if struck by a bolt of lightning the realization of what was happening hit him; he was going to make love for the first time to a real woman. Kelly then proceeded to take his clothes off as fast as possible. He fell over trying to take off his boots, this brought peals of laughter from Doris. Before he ran down to the water, he spread out the blanket beside the truck in preparation for what he was sure was going to come. By the time he got to the water Doris wasn't in sight. He called her name and she answered back from behind him. He snapped around to face her as she advanced on him. Doris put her finger to her mouth in a quiet signal and began to gently push him farther out into the water. When the water came up the about the middle of Kelly's thigh Doris launched herself at him and wrapped her arms around his neck. This caused Kelly to lose his balance and fall backwards into the water with Doris on top of him. Moments later they came back to the surface sputtering and coughing. In between coughs they both laughed hysterically.

"Are you trying to drown me or what?" Kelly asked as he finally got his feet back under him.

"No…not yet anyway. I want to make love to you first." Doris replied as she again launched herself at him.

This time he was ready and caught her. She wrapped her arms around his neck and began kissing him passionately. Kelly wasn't sure what to do so he accepted the passion and returned it with the same ardor. Soon his hands began to explore her body, with each touch she seemed to develop even more passion. When his hands moved across her breasts a small moan came from her lips and she whispered for him not to stop.

Soon he found them on the blanket by the truck and he wasn't sure how they got there…nor did he care. He was entwined in the arms of a woman and she was very receptive to his ministrations. With each touch of his hands or lips she would moan and try to get even closer to him.

Doris was just as busy as Kelly. She gently stroked his back and his chest. Then she worked her way slowly down to his manhood and took a firm grip on it. Suddenly she started pushing him over onto his back and climbed on top of him. As she came to a sitting position he could feel his manhood slip inside her. Doris slowly lowered herself down onto his manhood with tiny squeals and moans. She began to gyrate slowly giving Kelly sensations that he had never felt before.

"Hey Kelly…what the hell are you grinning at?" someone called to him snapping him out of his reverie.

"Damn, Manse…you just screwed up a beautiful memory." Kelly growled back. This brought laughter and catcalls from the rest of the team. The banter kept up until the door opened and Dick walked in carrying some rolled up maps.

"Hey Dick…we need to take Kelly down to the village and get him laid." Scuzzy Bill called out.

"Well, Kelly's sexual needs are going to have to wait. We have an important mission." Dick said as he cleared a space on the table and unrolled the maps. The men gathered around the table while Dick explained what was going on.

"Team three got caught in an ambush today and they got hit hard. Three wounded but none killed, since we are the only team available we're going in and clean up the mess. They were two klicks north and west of Phan Loy Duc when they got hit. But the good part is we now know who leaked the intel to the V.C." Dick reported. He went on to explain that it had to be My Ling, their hooch maid; because she was the only one around when the mission was discussed and the only one who understood enough English to make sense of what was being said.

Dick got out his plastic covered map and started showing the team the drop points and the extraction point. From there he outlined that this would be a kill mission. He looked over at Kelly and asked if he felt up to it. Kelly just nodded.

"Kelly tell me now if you don't think you can do it because once you pull the trigger you will be a changed man. I have to know for sure that you can do it." Dick said quietly.

For a long moment Kelly just looked Dick in the eyes and knew that he was serious. Then Kelly took what seemed like a long time to answer because he was turning over in his own mind if he could pull the trigger. Was shooting someone from far away murder or was it just a part of war? Did he have the detached frame of mind to do it? Would his religious upbringing keep him from pulling the trigger?

"I can do it. I have no doubt in my mind." Kelly said dropping his eyes from Dick's eyes.

"That's all I needed to hear from you." Dick said nodding his head. He then proceeded on with the briefing. As he was finishing up the briefing Pete came in with a distressed look on his face.

"What's up Pete?" Dick called to him.

"guys I've got some unwelcome news…Ben Clayton was killed this morning in the attack. Rob Collette and Jim Madden were badly wounded. We're going to disband team three until we can get some more qualified people in. This just means that you'll be busier than normal for the foreseeable future." Pete stated tiredly.

"Pete, you're not telling us everything; what aren't you saying?" Dick asked.

"Major Tau and the Forth Brigade have set up camp just over the border in Laos." Pete replied. This brought groans from all the men except Kelly who was operating in ignorance.

Major Tau and the Forth Brigade were a Viet Cong group with a very bloody reputation. Most of the villagers in the mountains along the border were afraid of him because of his heartless treatment of them. In several documented cases he had been the one who gave the order for several villages to be destroyed and their inhabitance murdered as a sign to the other villages of what would happen to them if they didn't cooperate with his forces. He was also suspected in the disappearance of two South Vietnamese Ranger teams. They were patrolling near the border and just disappeared. Rumors began to filter back from the area that they had been captured and killed, but their bodies were never found.

"So, does that mean he's now become target number one?" Dick asked. "No, our job is still intel; but if you get a shot at him take him out." Pete replied.

"It's going to be hard to get a shot at him if he stays in Laos, but then we could make a navigation error." Dick replied looking Pete straight in the eyes.

"I'm not saying to do that…but if it happens I don't think anyone will get shook up about it. You know what I mean?" Pete said. Everyone just nodded a silent understanding.

The members of Team Two now knew what was expected of them. Pete had told them without saying it that Major Tau was a priority target. From where they were being inserted and Major Tau's base camp was about three miles through some of the toughest jungles in Viet Nam. The team was very familiar with this area since they had been operating in it for about three months. But the team had an advantage, they didn't have to move around a lot to gather intel about troop movements.

They also had the element of anger on their side, since the ambush of Team Three they were now dead set on revenge. If they could sneak in and kill Major Tau without getting caught they would feel vindication not only for themselves but for the villagers as well.

"So now you guys know what's going on. All I can say is good luck." Pete said as he walked out the door. The team just watched him go in silence, no one said anything until the door slammed shut and then they all started talking at once. To Kelly they sounded like a flock of magpies. Suddenly Dick gave an ear-splitting whistle and all talk stopped.

"Alright you guys let's get back to the briefing." Dick said, "Now here's the tentative plan; we're being inserted on the east side of hill 245 and then we proceed around the north side into Vin Luc valley. We go west up the valley and go up hill 269, we conceal ourselves and wait. After the shot we'll go six klicks east to the extraction point at hill 211. Everyone understand?" Dick asked.

"What happens if we get separated?" Kelly asked. This question caused some snickers from the rest of the team members.

"Well...if that happens, you're on your own. But try to get over to one of the villages to the east. Most of them have a Vietnamese army detachment in them and they will help you get back here. But the best course of action is not to get separated in the first place." Dick snorted, "Now let's check our gear and get some rest; lift off is at 0700."

Kelly went back to his bunk and started checking his gear when he noticed that he hadn't finished reading his mail. He finished packing his rucksack and then picked up the letter he was getting ready to read before he was interrupted. Once again, he grinned wistfully as he stared at the handwriting on the envelope. He opened the envelope and pulled out the paper; he immediately got a whiff of Doris' perfume. His mind pictures her again and he feels a twinge of longing and loneliness just thinking about her. Kelly starts reading the normal "how are you, I'm fine. I miss you and wish you were here.". After that she wrote about the news from the people they both knew.

He finished reading the letter and put it away. He still had the feeling of emptiness that loneliness brings. He wished to himself that she was there to help him loose the feeling that he was alone. Even though he was with five other guys he felt like he was in a bubble and no one cared if he was there or not. Since he had returned to the company area after being wounded in the mortar attack he felt like he had no friends and was just a warm body taking up a space on the rooster.

But now that he had finally gotten some mail he didn't feel quite so alone. He realized that he had someone besides his family that thought about him. That thought made him feel better. As Kelly looked at the other team members he realized that what he was feeling was really fear. He didn't know if it stemmed from the fact that he was about to go out on his first mission or if it was from having been wounded. Not knowing what to expect during the mission only added to his sense of fear.

Perhaps, fear wasn't the right word for what he was feeling. He had been on many missions during training, but this wasn't training, and real life had a way of being totally different from what you're trained to do. The one thing he had learned was that you had to learn quickly to think on the fly. This is where the intribution came into play, could he make the right decision? Would he be called on to make the right decision? These were the kind of things that were running through his mind when Dick called for him and motioned for him to follow him outside.

"Kelly, I would like to think that we're friends and what I tell you is for your own good." Dick said, "Some of the guys have told me they're scared to go to the field with you because they think you might be jinxed. This first mission is going to be so important to dispel that kind of thinking."

"Dick, you and I both know that nonsense. I was just in the wrong place at the wrong time, I'm ready for this mission. I know I can do the job and I'm anxious to prove it." Kelly said in a plaintiff tone.

"Now, don't go getting your bowels in an uproar…I'm not scraping you for the mission. I just want you to be aware of what's being said, not that I believe any of it. But, guys in this job are very superstitious." Dick explained, "On this first mission you have to do things right to dispel their fears. Understand?"

"Yeah, I think I do...I've got to be better than anyone else or they'll never have trust in me. Is that about the size of it?" Kelly replied.

"Pretty much, do you still think you can do it?" Dick asked.

"Now more than ever, if I don't do it my butt is going to be shipped off to some line company and all the training I've had will be for naught and you know how I hate wasting things." Kelly said.

"That...my young Kelly is the kind of answer I was looking for." Dick said as he got up from the sandbags they had been sitting on. "Look to these guys for guidance in the field, they're all veterans and know what they're doing. Just follow their lead and you'll be fine." Kelly nodded and started back inside.

"Kelly This isn't anything you need to get in a funk about. I've known you for quite a while and I know what you can do, trust me this isn't anything to worry about." Dick said as he sauntered off towards the orderly room.

Kelly watched him go and his mind was alive with questions and self-doubt. "If these guys don't trust me how can I trust them?" Kelly thought, "If something goes wrong will they abandon me?" He didn't think they really would, but, in war many strange things happen and the truth of what happened doesn't come out until years later.

"Hey Kelly, we're dividing up the rations...you want to come in and pick out a favorite." Manse called. He went back inside but the conversation with Dick still nagged at the back of his mind, he was grateful for the distraction so that he didn't have to think about it.

# CHAPTER 4

*Try not to be a person of success,
But rather a person of value.*

*Albert Einstein
(1879-1955)*

In the far-off darkness the sound of artillery softly boomed from a firebase just a few miles from the encampment. Kelly had never seen nights so dark, the only illumination was the light from the stars. The stillness of the jungle had also been a surprise to him; he had thought that it would be full of sound like in the movies.

His biggest surprise had come earlier in the day when they got off the chopper. Instead of landing on solid ground the chopper hovered at the top of some elephant grass, when he stepped off the chopper he thought he was stepping onto solid ground but instead dropped about twelve feet before contacting the ground with a thud. Kelly landed with a grunt as the wind was knocked from his lungs. Seconds later Scuzzy Bill dropped down just a few feet from him.

Kelly quickly checked to make sure that he hadn't broken anything and then looked through the stems of the grass at Bill who was sitting there snickering at Kelly's obvious confusion.

"Elephant grass is a bitch." Was all he said. Kelly nodded emphatically.

As soon as the last man had jumped from the chopper it had left as fast as possible so as not to give away the position of the team. Everyone checked their gear and themselves to make sure nothing was broken. Manse took the lead and started hacking their way to where the grass met the jungle. It was only about two hundred yards, but it seemed to take forever to get out of the grass; they had to change a couple of times because of how tiring it was.

By the time they had hacked their way to the jungle's edge they had been dropped for three hours. After a short rest they began to climb an old water course strewn with boulders the size of a Volkswagen. It was a rough climb and they had to stop several times to rest. When they reached the top of the water course there was a trail that headed to the northeast; but according to their maps that wasn't the way they needed to go. What surprised them the most was that there were fresh boot tracks in the soft soil. From the depth of the tracks they could tell that each man was carrying a heavy load.

The tracks didn't look like they were American boots because they were smaller than most G.I. prints. They decided that to avoid a possible ambush they would go the opposite direction and then cut west at the next ridge. It was a lot easier walking the trail then it was coming up the water course. It was almost like walking on flat ground.

Each time they took a break to rest, Kelly would look around and was amazed at how lush and green the countryside was. "They didn't have anything like this back in Texas" he thought. The closest he had come to seeing anything like Viet Nam was the swamps over on the Louisiana border along the Sabine River. Those were mostly mangrove swamps but here he was in the mountains; that was a new experience for him.

He was used to seeing small rolling hills or just plain flatland studded with small pine forest or the occasional scrub oak. Seeing these towering trees and the forest that seemed to go on forever simply amazed him.

Suddenly Dick signaled for everyone to get off the trail. They all dove into the bush and crawled several feet back into the brush to hide. They did it as quickly and as quietly as possible. Kelly's heart was pounding, it felt like it was going to jump out of his chest. He was also very scared, what if someone saw them and started shooting. They were too close to the trail not to be killed by a large group.

As Kelly watched the trail he saw a person dressed in what could only be described as black silk pajamas and a flattened conical straw hat and carrying a rifle coming up the trail. The only odd thing about him was the leather pouch he carried slung across his body. He seemed to be in a hurry but didn't look back over his shoulder until it was too late. Manse had jumped behind him clamped his hand over his mouth. The man struggled for a few moments then went limp. Manse put him over his shoulder, picked up his hat and rifle and disappeared silently back into the brush.

A few minutes later a pebble hit Kelly in the back and he snapped his head in the direction he thought it had come. He saw Scuzzy Bill a few yards away motioning for him to follow him but also to be quiet. They crept a few more yards further from the trail and found Manse, the captive, Bumper, Slick and Dick huddled behind a boulder.

"We just got us a courier, Bumper I want you and Manse to carry this fool until we can get him picked up. Bill, you take point; head for the river when we get there I'll call for a slick. Slick you and Kelly bring up the rear." Dick said in a loud whisper. All the men nodded and proceeded to their assigned positions. In a few short minutes they were on their way.

Bill lead the way down the hill and at an angle away from the trail. In what seemed like no time at all they were on flat ground heading for a tree line. When they reached it, they set up a tight perimeter where they could see each other. After they had gotten settled in Dick broke radio silence, gave their coordinates and told them to come pick up a package. They then settled in to wait for the call on the radio telling them that the chopper was in-bound. During the wait they all spoke in very hushed tone since they didn't want anyone to know they were there. Kelly moved over beside Dick

"Is this going to change our mission?" Kelly asked.

"That I don't know…But Bronco one said he'd let us know." Dick replied. Then he noticed Slick waving the handset for the radio at him. Dick moved over and spoke into the handset. After a few minutes of conversation, he handed the handset back to Slick. He motioned for everyone to come over to where he was.

"Bronco one said we need to bring the package home, which means we're back to square one on our original mission." Dick explained as he looked at each man,

"Major Tau will get to live a little longer thanks to the fool over there." Dick said pointing his thumb at their prisoner.

The radio crackled again Slick acknowledged and then he said, "Mount up…birds are coming in." This announcement was followed by a flurry of activity as the men got back into their rucksacks in preparation to leave. In the distance they heard the choppers. Scuzzy Bill helped their prisoner to his feet, since he had his hands tied behind his back. He then pulled him along as they got into position for the extraction. When the chopper came into sight Slick popped a smoke grenade to mark the landing zone. With a lot of wind and noise the chopper set down just long enough for the six men and their prisoner to climb on; then they were up and away.

The trip back to base camp didn't take long but it did give Kelly enough time to get a look at the country side. He was amazed at how the natives had laid out the rice paddies. During this time of year, the paddies were dry; but Kelly couldn't imagine what it would look like when they were flooded for planting. He further couldn't imagine how they could get that much water into them. He would have to ask someone about that.

Kelly also found it amazing that the paddies ran right up to the base of the mountains to where the jungle took over. It was quite the contrast in color between the light brown and tan of the dry rice paddies and the lush green of the jungles. It seemed as if all the valley floors were taken up with rice paddies except for the tiny islands where they had built their homes. Around the houses there were trees that broke up the landscape so that the valley floors didn't seem so flat and they gave shade to the hooch's in the summertime which helped to keep them cool.

When they landed at base they were greeted by two Vietnamese Army officers who took charge of the prisoner. They were going to escort him to a prisoner of war camp where he would be questioned and the documents in the pouch examined. The officer in charge expressed thoughts that maybe they could get an idea of what the enemy was planning if they could make the captive talk.

The team watched as they drove away, then Slick said, "I sure am glad I'm not that man."

"Why is that?" Kelly asked.

"Well for one thing he's about to get his ass kicked up between his shoulders. If he's lucky that's all they'll do to him." Slick replied.

"But what about the Geneva Convention? Doesn't that say that they can't abuse him to get him to talk?" Kelly asked. This brought chuckles from the rest of the team.

"Kelly, I understand that you're new here, so I'll explain it to you. First, South Viet Nam is not a signer to the agreement. Second, these people don't view life the same way we westerners do; they think life is a cheap commodity and if a prisoner dies while being interrogated then that's just too bad." Dick said.

This shocked Kelly. He couldn't understand how people could think of life in those terms. He had always been taught that life was precious and should be preserved as much as possible. Was it because of their religion or was it something else that made them think like that. He found this very confusing. He couldn't understand how his team members could be so cavalier about someone going to be tortured or worse. He wondered if in time he would become as callous as his new friends seemed to be. Kelly made up his mind right then and there that he would try his best to remember that people and life were precious.

Kelly remembered several conversations he had with his father about how war could change a person. His father had served with Patton's Third Armor in France during World War II. He cautioned Kelly not to become complacent when it came to the loss of life. He had told him that when he had seen large numbers of people killed that the human psyche becomes numb to the horror of war. He had said that he prayed that Kelly would remember that his enemy was still a human being and deserved respect.

While Kelly stood trying to wrap his mind around this new perspective, a three-quarter ton jeep pulled up. As the men were slugging into their rucksacks, Pete stuck his head out the window and inquired if anyone was needing a ride. The men heartily agreed and piled all their gear in the back and then followed it. They were soon bouncing along the rutted road that lead to the company compound. When they reached the compound, Dick told them to put their gear away and then meet him in Pete's office.

"OK Bill...what have you done now?" someone called.

"I ain't done nothing...I've been with you guys for the last three days." Bill replied.

"Well, if it isn't you then who else could it be?" Slick said. After a few moments they all turned and looked at Kelly.

"Wasn't me!" Kelly said in a plaintive tone.

"If it wasn't you or Scuzzy Bill then one of us is in trouble for something we didn't even know we did." Manse said.

The team finished putting away their gear and headed over to the orderly room to meet Dick and Pete. As they walked along they speculated on what could be going on. They each tried to recall what misadventure had finally caught up to them. No one could think of any serious infraction of the rules that would cause the entire team to be called on the carpet. The last thing they had done was to make a class six depot raid with fake requisition orders.

When they walked into the orderly room Bill told them to stand by while he let Pete know that they had arrived. When he went into Pete's office, Manse saw Colonel Wilburn sitting in the chair beside Pete's desk. This made him worry because Colonel Wilburn didn't come around unless someone was in serious trouble or was being awarded. Now he was wondering which it was going to be and who it was going to be. He quietly told the rest of the team what he has seen, this brought groans of trepidation from the rest of the team.

Colonel Jackson Wilburn came from a distinguished military family, he had relatives in every war since the revolutionary war. He had graduated tenth in his class at West Point and served with distinction under General Omar Bradley during world war II. He was then assigned to the Japanese Reconstruction Command until Korea broke out. There he commanded a rifle company with the 1st Cavalry.

After being wounded he was sent to Tokyo to recover. There he met a young officer whom he became friends with; a fellow named Pete Philmore. Pete started talking about what he did, and it intrigued him so much that he decided to get more information. After he found out about what the long-range recon teams did he decided that he wanted to be a part of it. He called in some favors and was sent to the Intelligence Analysis School at Ft. Belvoir, Virginia.

After graduating at the top of his class he was assigned to the Pentagon and did analysis of the situation in South Viet Nam. When he complained that his intel about troop movements was too old to matter. As a result, he was assigned to MACV G-2 group. There he got his intel as fresh as possible. When Pete was assigned to the 75th Ranger Battalion, he immediately had him assigned to his own company.

Now he had come to see Pete for some good news instead of collecting a dead soldier's personal effects. He was here to promote two people; these were the kind of assignments he enjoyed. When he gets see the expression on their faces, it makes him feel good inside.

In the ante room the six men were mulling over what misadventure had come to the attention of the Battalion Commander. They knew that if he had made a personal visit that it couldn't be good. As far as they could figure out they hadn't done anything that warranted this visit.

"Guys, Pete says to come on in." Bill said. The six men got up and headed for the door.

"Hey Bill, do you know what's going on?" Dick asked.

"All I know is that Pete told me to come find you when you got in and have you and the team come to his office." Bill replied.

"That isn't much help you know." Dick said with a glower. "Sorry Captain, that's the best I can do." Bill countered.

The six men walked into Pete's office, formed a line, saluted and Dick said, "Team two reporting as requested, sir." Pete and Colonel Wilburn returned the salute and looked at each one. "Sargent Mansger why are you out of uniform?" Cornel Wilburn asked.

Manse franticly searched his uniform trying to find what the colonel was talking about.

"Sir, I can't find anything the Colonel could be referring to." Manse barked back.

"Mansger, you're a staff Sargent, is that correct?" Cornel Wilburn asked. "Yes sir." Manse replied.

"Wrong!" Colonel Wilburn exclaimed. Manse stiffen knowing something bad was coming. "Mansger you are no longer a staff sergeant…you are now a second lieutenant."

It took a few moments for what Colonel Wilburn has said to sink in and he began to smile. His feeling of dread quickly changed to one of elation. He wanted to jump with joy; but, military decorum didn't allow it.

"Sergeant Broadwick!" Colonel Wilburn barked. "Yes sir!" Kelly replied sharply.

"You have been in country about two and a half months, is that correct?" Colonel Wilburn asked.

"Yes sir, that's correct." Kelly replied rigidly.

"And you have already collected up a purple heart, is that also correct?" the Colonel continued. Kelly nodded. "Well, since we have promoted Mansger to second Lieutenant, that leaves an E-6 slot unfilled. The only way we can fill it is to promote you to E-6; so, consider it done." Kelly smiled to himself.

"Gentlemen…You're dismissed. We will reconvene at the refrigerator where we'll drink a toast to your promotions." Pete said. The congratulations started flowing between the team members with Pete and Colonel Wilburn heartily joined in. The conversation was lively, but Kelly got the feeling that it was somewhat constrained.

Maybe it was just him, after all to these men he was an unknown entity. The only person who had known him before he became part of the unit was Dick Van Meter. They had gone through basic training and advanced infantry training together. Kelly didn't feel exactly ostracized, but at the same time he didn't feel as if he were a part of the group. Maybe as time went on and they got to know him this feeling would go away.

"Gentlemen, the time has come for us to get down to some bona fide business." Colonel Wilburn announced after a brief time, "Shall we adjourn to the map table where we can discuss your next mission." With that the group moved over to the table in the corner that had several maps spread out on it.

"Gentlemen I can't stress too much the importance of this and several more missions to come. We have intel that the North Vietnamese are moving massive quantities of men and material down the Ho Chi Mien trail. We need to know what they're moving and how big the convoys are. On this mission you are not to engage the enemy, fire only in defense and then get the hell out of there." Colonel Wilburn explained.

"How creditable are the reports we've already gotten?" Manse asked. "Well they came from the green beret camp at An Lin." Colonel Wilburn replied.

"Then we're just going in to confirm what's already been reported, is that correct?" Slick asked.

"Yes, that's correct. But I can't stress to you how important it is that you not engage them. If they know that we're on to them, then they'll move their operation over into Laos and Cambodia where we can't touch them." Pete said.

"So, what's the plan Colonel?" Dick asked.

"We're going to lift your team to An Lin and you'll scout the area with the green berets for a few days. Then you'll set up an observation post above the trail and document what you see. At the end of a week, if you haven't been discovered, you'll go back to An Lin and be lifted back here." Colonel Wilburn said.

"And if we're discovered?" Dick asked.

"Then you fight your way out and beat feet back to An Lin. If need be you'll get air support, but the important thing is to get back. We need that intel." Colonel Wilburn stated.

"This almost sounds like a suicide mission, Colonel." Scuzzy Bill said. "Oh, this is far from that, you men are not expendable. If we can figure out what the N.V.A. and Viet Cong are up to then we can prepare for it. By doing this you could save many American and South Vietnamese lives." Colonel Wilburn explained.

"Colonel…if we get a chance to snatch an officer, should we?" Manse asked.

"Absolutely not!" the colonel said emphatically, "This is an observation only mission…and that's all. Do you gentlemen understand that?" The team members all nodded their understanding. After a few more operational questions, the team was dismissed to go and celebrate the promotions at the compound club.

# CHAPTER 5

*You will suffer and you will hurt*
*You will have joy and you will have peace*

*Alison Cheek*
*(1927-?)*

Slowly the compound came to life in the early morning sunshine. The smells and sounds were now commonplace to Kelly as he and his team mates continued their celebration of the promotions that had been bestowed on them the previous evening.

Soon after the team had arrived at the club, they were joined by Pete and Colonel Wilburn. As the evening progressed, the barriers between senior officers and enlisted personnel came down and they acted more like a bunch of friends getting together after work. There were jokes and the use of first names and no mention of rank. By the end of the evening a firm bond had been forged between the team and Colonel Wilburn. This was something the colonel had been hoping for, the reputation that team two had was as a can-do team had impressed him very much. It was important for Jackson Wilburn to be able to believe in the people he worked with. From what he had seen of team two, they were very close knit and as ready to die for one another as any group of men he had ever worked with.

When breakfast was finished the company clerk began distributing the mail to the teams that were still in the compound. When he got to team two's hooch he was surprised to see that any of them were even out of bed yet. He handed each man his mail and moved on the next team.

Each man became immediately totally engrossed in his letters. It didn't matter if they were from family, friends, wife or girlfriend, it was a reminder of what awaited them when they left Viet Nam. In some letters there were pictures some were of babies and some were of get-togethers. But no matter what the pictures were of they were always welcomed. Suddenly Kelly jumped up and started cussing, this took the team by surprise.

"What's the matter Kelly?" Dick asked.

"Doris...she's dumping me for some clown at the drive-in where she works!" Kelly exclaimed, "I'll kill the little bastard!"

"Just calm down...there isn't anything you can do about it and getting mad isn't going to solve anything." Dick replied.

"That's easy for you to say...you're married to your girl." Kelly shot back. "Maybe so, but I've had women dump me before and getting mad never solved anything." Dick countered.

"Dick's right Kelly, you're over here and she's back in the world. There isn't a whole lot you can do but forget about it and hope the next one treats you better." Scuzzy Bill said.

"Yeah...I know. But it still stinks...how am I supposed to get over this? I thought we really had something and now she dumps me." Kelly replied as a forlorn look crossed his face.

"I've got an idea...write a letter to her but put in some other girl's name in the greeting. Make the letter all mushy and stuff. Knowing that you're writing that sweet stuff to someone else and she can't do anything about it will drive her crazy." Scuzzy Bill said with an evil grin. After a few moments Kelly began to grin.

"Bill...you're an evil little bastard. But I like it" Kelly said starting to laugh.

This began a discussion of other girlfriends the other team members had before the ones they were currently with. Each one related stories of things they had done and situations they had gotten caught in. Some of them were funny as could be; like Bill and his girlfriend skinny-dipping and being caught by the game warden. Others were more tragic; like Slick having his girlfriend run away with his best man on the day they were supposed to get married. These various stories didn't help with Kelly's anger, but they did make him realize that he wasn't the first soldier to get dumped by the girl he loved.

Kelly set about composing the letter; he started with "Dear Sophia". He knew that if Doris really cared about him this would drive her crazy and she would immediately stop her relationship with that guy from work. If she didn't really care about him, it's a good thing he found out about it now instead of a few years down the road. But, it still made him feel like he was alone and that nobody cared about his pain.

The door opened, and the company clerk stuck his head in and said that Pete wanted the whole team in his office in ten minutes. The only reason Pete would call for the entire team was to brief them on a mission. Everyone looked at each other, they weren't scheduled to go back out for another three days. This could only mean that one of the other teams had gotten into trouble. This thought was depressing because they didn't know who got into trouble or where they got into it. Immediately they started speculating on who it was and where they might be.

Kelly immediately forgot about his letter and put it away. Now he had more important business to attend to. The thought of going back into the field excited Kelly. Not because there might be a fight, but rather because it'll be another chance for him to prove to the other team members that they could trust him to do his job. Gaining the trust of these men was very important to Kelly because he knew that at any time they may be called on to save his life, just as he may be called on to save theirs.

The team left the hooch and headed towards Pete's office; they were still speculating about the who's and the where's. But Dick put an end to it by stating they find out soon enough. This didn't satisfy Slick since he was the worrier of the team. He continued with his speculating until Dick turned around and got nose to nose with him; he then told him to shut his mouth or Dick would shut it for him. The sudden confrontation was uncharacteristic of Dick and left the rest of the team uneasy. They weren't used to Dick being short tempered; he was generally tolerant of mistakes. So, when he blew up it surprised the team and they knew he was worried about what this meeting meant. They then continued in silence.

When they entered the orderly room, the clerk waved them on in to Pete's office. As they enter they see Pete standing by the map table with a disturbed look on his face. He looked up as the team filed in; he then waved them over to the map table, after they were gathered around it he began. "Gentlemen...that prisoner that you brought back has been singing his heart out. He's given us locations and routes and all sorts of intel. The pouch he was carrying held a treasure trove of intel about their command structure. We're in the process of getting photos of the commanders so that we can pick them off." Pete said as he scratched his head.

"Pete...you're not telling us all of it. What aren't you telling us?" Dick asked. Pete ran his hand through his hair and looked each man in the eye.

"Well Dick...team six got wiped out this morning." Pete replied. The team reacted with stunned silence.

"What happened?" Dick asked quietly.

"From what we have been able to piece together they were on an observation post and were discovered. They got hit about sun up and we lost contact about three hours later." Pete explained.

"Where were they?" Manse asked.

"They were over on the border on hill three seventy-two. They were watching the Ho Chi Minh trail trying to verify what your prisoner had said." Pete said.

"How did they get there?" Kelly asked.

"They were dropped in three klicks east and settled in at dark." Pete replied.

"Then it sounds to me like we have a leak here at home." Kelly speculated. "Yes Kelly, I would tend to agree with you. But I thought when we arrested that hooch maid, we had sealed the leak. OK guys...From now on no one speaks of their missions out of this room." Pete said in a frustrated tone. "Billy...tell all the squad leaders that are in camp I want to see them immediately." Billy called back an affirmative answer and rushed out the door.

"Do you think that'll solve it?" Dick asked.

"I sure hope so, I don't want any more occurrences like todays." Pete replied. After looking at each man he went on to outline the team's mission. They were to take up an observation post one klick north of where team six got hit and observe the Ho Chi Minh trail for signs of activity. They were to be silent, that meant no radio traffic except for emergency traffic. They could report on what they saw when they got back. Nor were they to engage the enemy. If they were discovered, they were to fight their way out as quickly as possible. Otherwise they were to stay in place for two nights and then fall back to the extraction point.

"What about team six?" Dick asked. It was the question that was on everyone's mind, but they didn't want to ask it.

"A company from America's Eleventh Brigade is going in to retrieve the bodies. They're the closest and most available." Pete said.

"I hope it's not the first of the twentieth, they have trouble finding their way out of a paper bag." Dick said quietly. This brought snickers from the other team members.

"No, it's not 1/20th…I think it's 4/21st" Pete replied. With the business of the mission completed, Pete dismissed the team and made sure they understood their instructions not to talk about it anywhere except in his office. Pete knew all too well that he needed to write letters to the families of the men who had been killed but it was something he hated to do. As he watched the team leave he wondered if he was going to have to write those same letters to their families at some time in the future.

The team made their way back to their hooch with a pallor of sadness and fear. They all knew that at any time, on any mission, it could be their families that were receiving the letter from Pete. The thought of his family receiving one of those letters made Kelly think of his father and how he might react. Kelly could see his father tightly hugging his mother and crying deep soul-racking sobs, while his mother was holding just as tightly to him and wailing her pain. This was something the very thought of made him feel even more depressed then what he felt already.

The team began to quietly get their gear ready for the mission. This included cleaning their rifles, checking their rucksacks to ensure that their food was in them and checking their spare rifle magazines. The team went through the motions of their work quietly each man lost in his own thoughts. After receiving such unwelcome news as they had this afternoon, each man was trying to carry on like nothing had happened; when down deep inside they really wanted to scream. They had lost friends that would not be coming back. Guys that they had drank with and done so many other things with. They all wanted to morn but there wasn't time for that since they had a mission to complete. The men put their grief aside and buried it deep inside where they could deal with it at some other time.

As with any warrior these men knew that the fate of Team Six could have been their fate. They were relieved that it wasn't but at the same time it made them angry that it had happened at all. Kelly remembered Clint Moss and Greg French as the two men who picked him up and carried him to the bunker that first day during the mortar attack. Now he would never get the chance to say thank you for bringing him out of harm's way. Should he write to their families and tell them what their sons had done, or should he just keep his thank you to himself. These deaths just angered him more and more to a point where he didn't care which enemy soldier he killed he just wanted revenge.

The quiet of the hooch was disturbed by the tinkle of small rain drops as they fell on the corrugated tin roof. Each man looked at the other, they all, except Kelly, knew what it meant; the monsoons were starting. It was late October and the rainy season was making its appearance. For the next several months they could expect rain every day and later in the season it was going to rain for days on end. Several of the men expressed their displeasure with expletives of disgust. Kelly couldn't understand why everyone was angry because of the rain; but as he was soon to find out, it meant rain that seemed to never end. When the men had finished their preparations, they realized it was time for dinner. When they had finished eating they made their way back to the hooch turned the lights down low and went to bed early.

With the rain and the news of team six no one felt much like doing anything. The blanket of sadness that covered the team was made complete by the knowledge of what awaited them in the field. For at least the next two days they would not be dry or comfortable; they would be moving through a wet jungle, sleeping on wet ground and eating cold food. They would not be able to take revenge for the loss of their friends which just added to their frustration. Kelly made a vow to himself that he would get even with those bastards.

As he lay in his bunk on the edge of sleep, Kelly thought about how satisfying it would be to get an N.V.A. officer in his sights. He didn't think about the pain it would cause the officers family; all he cared about was revenge. When he examined what he was thinking it shocked him. He had never been one to seek revenge for anything, but now it was all he could think about. In training they had taught him not to think of the enemy as anything but a target, now he was thinking of them as even less than a target. But he couldn't understand where the change had occurred. Was it when he was wounded or maybe when he heard the news about team six. Either way he had changed but that was one of the side effects of war. A wise man once said that the first casualty of war was innocence, Kelly figured that he had just become another casualty of war. His last thought before drifting off to sleep was how would his Dad react to this change in him.

At 0600 the next morning Billy, the company clerk, came in and woke them up for breakfast. After breakfast they changed into their "tiger striped' fatigues that they wore in the jungle. They checked their gear one more time and then headed down to the helipad for their flight to the drop-off point. When they arrived at the helipad there was an ambulance waiting. Soon they heard the woop-woop of helicopter blades as a huey slick set down. The men from the ambulance rushed to the chopper and unloaded two body-bags, put them into the ambulance and went back to the chopper for the other two bags. With the unloading complete, the pilot signaled for the team to get aboard.

The unloading of the bodies and the loading of the team had only taken a few minutes but to Kelly it seemed like a long time. Before he knew it, they were airborne and flying through low clouds and mist. In what seemed like a blink of an eye the chopper was setting down in a dry rice paddy and the team scrambled off. Just as quickly as it had come the chopper was gone; all that could be heard was the faint popping of the rotor blades in the distance.

As soon as the chopper was gone the team headed for the cover of the trees at the edge of the paddy. They quickly huddled to get their bearings and then moved out across the rice paddy towards the hills to the west. They moved along rapidly to lessen the chance of being sighted by the enemy. When they reached the tree line they slowed their pace to minimize any noise they made. They continued through the wet jungle for about two hours taking short breaks along the way. At various times Dick would consult the map and give direction to whomever was walking point. After what seemed like most of the day, they came to a point that over looked a narrow valley where a dirt road could clearly be seen. They pulled back into the trees so as not to be seen and settled in to wait for whatever came down the road.

They didn't have to wait long, they heard before they saw a large convoy of trucks bouncing along the road. From the way they rocked even a blind man could see that they were heavily loaded. Kelly counted twenty-seven trucks each with two armed guards walking beside them. Out of his rucksack Dick had produced a camera and he got pictures of the convoy. They could tell by the dress that these men they were watching were North Vietnamese Army regulars.

After the convoy had moved on Dick had commented that he had never seen that many trucks at one time and that something must be brewing. This began a quiet discussion of what might possibly be in the works. As far as command knew, there had been no indication of an offensive. But the more they discussed what they had seen, the more convinced they were that something big was going to be happening soon. As they were discussing the trucks, Scuzzy Bill made a motion for quiet; then pointed back towards the road. None of the team could believe what they were seeing, a column of men that stretched at least a quarter of a mile. They were all well-armed and marching in formation, one line down each side of the road. After they had passed the team compared notes and came up with a figure of about three hundred soldiers, now they knew for certain something big was in the air.

The only American position this far west was the Marine fire base at Khe Son. It was a good-sized base and for the NVA to take it would be very demoralizing. But then there was also the First Air Cavalry base at Dak To, for them to over-run that base would be equally demoralizing. These were places Kelly had never heard of, but he was learning. Being the "new guy" was quite a departure from what Kelly was used to; he was used to being the one with all the information and knew what to do. He was quickly realizing that there was a lot for him to learn and not much time for him to learn it.

Just as he thought he had learned a lesson, fate threw something new at him. He wasn't sure what scared him more dying or the thought of being the cause of someone else dying because of his ignorance. These thoughts made him shiver, but it also helped him solidify his resolve to not be the cause of someone's death and to learn as much as he could as quickly as he could. To have the guilt that he was the cause of someone's death hanging over his head would be more than he could bear.

After a second convoy had passed and things became quiet again, the men again began musing about what could be in the offing. Bumper made the comment that the Christmas truce was coming up and Slick said that Tet was just around the corner. Kelly listened intently to the conversation trying to learn as much as he could. He asked what Tet was and Dick explained that it was the Vietnamese new year celebration. This was something that Kelly didn't understand, new year's was on January first. Then Dick explained that the Buddhist calendar was different from the western calendar because of the Chinese started to keep track of time before western civilization did. As a result, their new year's celebration is on a different day then the western one. Tet was usually the end of January or in early February. This seemed very strange to Kelly; but he was learning.

For the next day they watched and counted several convoys as they passed. It seemed unnerving to allow that many soldiers pass without lifting a finger to stop them. But that was their orders; they were not to engage, only watch and information about the size and type of armament that was being moved. Since the mission was only for three days it was necessary for the team to pull back to a safe point for extraction. On the third morning Dick told them to get ready to move. After about four hours of walking they reached a clearing at the top of a ridge. They stayed back in the tree line while bumper called for the chopper to pick them up. Soon they heard the tell-tale sound of a chopper in the distance. When instructed to by the chopper pilot, Dick tossed a red smoke grenade out into the open. Within minutes the team was safely on-board and headed back to base camp.

When they arrived at the chopper pad at basecamp they found, Billy, the company clerk, who told Dick that Pete needed to see him immediately and for the rest of the team to go back to their hooch.

"Something going on Billy?" Dick asked.

"Don't know…Pete got a call from H.Q. this morning and then he started stomping around his office like a madman." Billy replied.

"That doesn't sound good." Was all Dick said as he got in the jeep and they roared off towards the orderly room. As soon as they arrived Pete called for Dick to come into his office.

"Morning Pete…what's going on?" Dick asked

"Well for one thing we've lost another team. Team one got hit this morning on their way to an observation post just south of where you guys were. We haven't been able to raise them on the radio for the last four hours. They had the same instructions you and your guys had; watch but don't engage. From what H.Q. told me they walked into an ambush and were fighting their way out." Pete explained.

"Jim Spanner was a good friend of mine and a good team leader, he would have gotten his guys out of there if he could. Did H.Q. say anything about how big a force they had run into?" Dick asked.

"No, but I don't think Jim and his crew even knew how big a force they were up against. The last communication said that they were going to move to the pick-up point and try to set up a perimeter. Whether they made it or not nobody knows. When the choppers got there no one was there, so we can only assume they didn't make it. That's why I have to send you and your guys back out immediately." Pete said. Pete held up his hand to stop Dicks protests. "You're the only team I've got. What I want you to do is get a couple hours sleep and then we'll get you guys back in here for a debrief and then we'll work it out from there."

"You know the guys aren't going to be happy. Especially Bumper, his cousin was on Spanner's team." Dick said, "How are they getting their information?"

"I wish I knew. I thought we had the leak plugged when we got that hooch maid. The only thing I can think to do now is to not allow any Vietnamese on our compound." Pete replied, "Why don't you leave Bumper behind, the family may want him to escort the body home."

"Pete…don't you think you're putting the cart before the horse? We don't know for sure they're dead." Dick said. Pete just looked at him over the rim of his reading glasses.

Dick shook his head and walked out. All the way back to the hooch he was trying to think of how to tell the team what had happened. Then he thought of bumper, this was going to be hard on him. Him and his cousin were quite close. As Dick approached the hooch, he decided the best way to handle it would be to come straight out with it and be prepared for Bumper to go to pieces.

Dick walked through the door and looked around, the only one in the hooch was Bumper. This is good Dick thought, now he could tell Bumper and prepare him for what might be coming. Dick hated to have to give bad news to any of his guys, especially ones that he had been with for a while. Bumper was always the easy going one of the bunch, not a whole lot got him upset except when he lost a lot at a poker game.

"Bumper… I've got some news that you're not going to like." Dick started, "Team one got hit this morning and H.Q. hasn't been able to raise them for the last four hours."

Bumper sat for a moment nodding his head; then asked, "What happened?"

"Well from what Pete told me, the information he got from H.Q. was that they walked into an ambush on their way to their extraction point. The last anyone heard was that they were going to set a perimeter and get ready for extraction. But when the choppers got there nobody was home.

At this point, H.Q. is assuming they're all dead but they're sending our team in to recover the remains. Because of your cousin being on team one, I'm forced to leave you behind because we don't want you going to pieces in the field, understand?" Dick said watching Bumpers reaction.

Bumper sat for a few more moments with his head in his hands. Then his great shoulders began to bounce as he quietly began to sob. These were sobs born of a heart so broken that tears were the only release for the pain. Dick put his arm around Bumper's shoulders and held on to him hoping that it would help to ease the pain. But deep in his heart he knew that only time would heal him. These were the times that nothing he learned in command school could help, all he could do was be the friend Bumper would need to get through such a great loss.

Dick heard the rest of the team coming back so he jumped up and headed out the door to cut them off and give Bumper some private time to deal with this great blow.

When Dick got outside he saw Kelly, Slick and Scuzzy Bill coming up the small dirt strip that served as a street between the canvas hooch's. He waved at them and motioned for quiet and was greeted with a look of bewilderment.

"Look guys, I just had to give Bumper some rough news so go away for a while and give him some time to digest it. O.K.?" Dick said quietly

"What kind of bad news? Did one of his folks pass away?" Slick asked. "No...well I might as well go ahead and tell you; Team one got hit this morning and H.Q. doesn't think there are any survivors." Dick sighed. The news was greeted with gawks of disbelief and exclamations of anger. A pallor of sadness quickly fell over the members of the team as Dick went on to explain what Pete had told him. "Why don't you guys go up to the PX for a while and let Bumper pull himself back together. When you get back get a couple hours sleep then when Pete has all the intel I'll wake you up and we'll get the skinny together."

"O.K. Dick," Slick replied, "If there is anything we can do for Bumper just let us know." With that they all turned and headed off to the PX.

Their shoulders were down, and anyone could see that they had been deeply touched by the news. They spoke very softly speculating on what the ambush on team one and what they had seen meant. Were they somehow connected? Was this the fate that awaited them on their next mission? That was a question only time would answer. The men began to speculate on how their families would receive the news of their being wounded or killed. It suddenly became a hotly debated topic and became apparent that this was not a topic they should be discussing. They were soon walking together in silence, each lost in his own thoughts. So much so that they walked right past the PX and out onto the beach. Here they sat down and in the shade of a palm tree drifted off to sleep.

# CHAPTER 6

*Everything is very simple in war,*
*But the simplest thing is difficult.*
*These difficulties accumulate and*
*Produce a friction no man can imagine*
*Exactly who has not seen war.*

Karl Von Clausewitz
1780-1831

The quietness of the jungle was very unnerving to the team as they slowly made their way toward the last known position of Team one. The jungle without the normal noises of the birds and small animals seemed much like a tomb. Even the shade of the trees seemed to close in on them. To add to the feeling the breeze had gone still and this in turn made the heat that much more oppressive. Suddenly Slick, who was walking point, stopped and started sniffing the air. He then knelt down as a sign for the other men to join him.

"Do you smell that?" he asked in a loud whisper. The other men began to sniff the air and made faces indicating disgust.

"How much further do you figure we have to go?" Scuzzy Bill asked.

"I would figure no more than a few hundred yards. Why are you asking a question like that?" Dick asked.

"Well, we smell death and I don't think it's a dead animal, for one thing. And for another the breeze is so light that the odor wouldn't carry that far. So maybe you need to rethink the distance." Bill explained. Dick looked at him very thoughtfully for a moment.

"You're right Bill, we need to spread out a little and see what we can find." Dick commanded. With that the team went in different directions out about one hundred yards looking for any sign of a fight.

When they all congregated back at the original point each one reported what he had found. Bill and Dick said they hadn't seen anything to indicate that anyone had walked the same area. Slick returned with news that he had found the trail of what seemed like a good-sized force moving parallel to the trail they were on. This made all the men nervous, were they about to walk into the same fate that team one had walked into.

"Ok, we'll move over to their trail and see where it leads. But everyone be alert." Dick ordered. "Slick you're a good tracker, you stay on point." With that they moved out in the direction of the trail Slick had found.

Slowly the team made their way across the valley and started up a small rise. They became more aware of the stench of rotting flesh. Mixed in with the stench was the smell of gunpowder. The team now knew they were getting close to the site of the battle. They moved even more cautiously now because they didn't know if there were still Viet Cong in the area. As they moved, they saw more trampled grass. When they saw the first body they stopped to examine it.

The body had been stripped of its weapons and left to rot. Kelly found this very strange. He had always been taught that you bury the dead and care for the wounded. But the mentality of his enemy seemed to be that the body wasn't important, but his weapons were. He assumed that this was just part of their religion. A religion he didn't understand.

After a careful examination of the body the team moved on towards the crest of the hill. Twice more they found bodies that were twisted and laying in grotesque shapes. They seemed to be following a trail of bodies. As they reached the top of the hill the foul odor of rotting corpses became almost nauseating. For now, everywhere they looked there were dead bodies. Kelly had seen blood before and smelled death before, but to see the bodies torn apart by the weapons of war was almost more than he could stand; it was something he was not prepared for. From the number of bodies lying about they could see that team one had put up one hell of a fight. The torn-up vegetation and the shattered trees told them that they had found team one's last position.

At Dick's direction they started searching the bodies trying to locate the members of team one. It seemed somehow disrespectful to search the bodies of the dead. But, this was war and all's fair in love and war. They took every scrap of paper they found on the bodies so that they could be deciphered and whatever intel was there could be extracted. Kelly paused as he came to one body, it was the body of a young boy who couldn't have been more than twelve or thirteen. What was such a young kid doing amid all this destruction. He couldn't understand how a parent could allow their son to join the army at such a young age.

"Hey Kelly…did you find something?" Dick quietly called to him. "No…not really it's a young kid lying dead. I just don't get it; why is he here?" Kelly replied.

"Well, for one thing, the mind of the far east works different than ours. They feel that this life is just a transition to a higher life. It's part of the Buddhist belief that you are reincarnated when you die and depending on what kind of life you lead determines what you come back as." Dick explained. Then gesturing around, them he joked, "These guys will probably come back as mosquitos to bother us even more." This brought a smile and a slight chuckle from Kelly.

They continued to search the bodies and Kelly couldn't believe the carnage he was seeing. His guess, without counting, was that there were about thirty bodies. The scene more resembled something Hollywood would put in a world war two movie. Before he could finish his thought, he heard a groan from a body close to him and then an arm started to move. A faint call of 'help' reached his ears and he immediately sprang to the side of one of the members of team one. As he moved he called for help and that he had found someone alive.

The man was covered in blood and dirt and resembled something that had climbed out of a grave. He was trying to get up and move but Kelly told to lie still as he called for Slick to bring the medic bag. Kelly gave him small sips of water which seemed to help. He was mumbling incoherently about something Kelly didn't understand. When Dick got to the spot, Kelly told him what the man had said before passing out.

"You're sure he said 'tong'?" Dick asked.

"Yeah, ask Slick, he heard him. All he said was tong; what does that mean?" Kelly asked, Slick nodded his agreement.

"I don't know...it might be the group that attacked them, or it could be the name of someone he recognized. Until we can talk to him more we can only guess at what he's trying to tell us." Dick replied thoughtfully.

While Slick ministered to the man's wounds, they were able to identify the man as being Greg Gleason. Meanwhile, the rest of the team continued to search the bodies. They were able to locate three more bodies as they found them they were placed them in body bags for transport to graves registration, where they would be identified, tagged and prepared for transport back home. The act of zipping up a body bag chilled Kelly so much that he shivered. He had seen dead bodies before, but this was the first time he had ever had to touch one and it shook him to his core. After they had gotten the bodies in the bags they lined them up near the crest of the hill and waited for the chopper.

He had never seen the results of what a bullet could do the human body and now he was face to face with these results. Kelly stood off to the side for a few moments trying not to throw up. As he stood there he noticed something odd; a faint trail of pressed down grass that headed towards the Woodline.

"Hey Dick" he softly called. Dick moved over to where he was standing, and Kelly pointed towards the trail he had discovered. "Something has been dragged down there through the grass."

"You're right, why don't you and Scuzzy Bill check it out. But be careful we don't know if the N.V.A. are still in the area." Dick replied. Kelly nodded his agreement.

Kelly and Scuzzy Bill picked up their rifles and started moving towards the tree line. They had only gone about fifty yards when they came upon another body, they could tell by the uniform that this one was one of the missing members of team one. He had cuts and stab wounds all over his back and he was lying face down. When they turned him over they recognized him as Bumper's cousin, James Spanner. This left only one more member to find and their hopes of finding him alive were dwindling by the minute.

Dick was still standing were they had left him; watching the progress they made down towards the tree line. They signaled for him to come to them and bring a body bag. They could see by the look on his face that Dick was disappointed. Dick called for Mense to stay with Gleason and for Slick to bring a body bag. When Mense arrived the four men carefully and gently placed Lt. Spanner's body in the bag and zipped it up. A pallor of sadness came over the men as this mission had turned into a very gruesome affair. The thought of having to fill one more body bag was almost more than Dick could handle. He had to do this too many times over the last five months and they didn't seem any closer to the source of the leak of intel than they were before.

The four men picked up the body bag and carried it back to where they had placed the other three. After they had set it down Dick told Bill and Kelly to continue on with their part of the mission. Both men just nodded and moved back to where they had found Lt. Spanner's body. As they went, Bill mumbled about how he hated going on recovery missions. When they reached the spot where Spanner's body had been, they searched around for clues as to whether Spanner had been alone or with someone. As they moved out from the spot Kelly noticed a small blood trail. He softly called for Bill to join him, when Bill arrived he pointed out the trail and then he noticed a smudge of blood on a tree several yards away. They moved carefully in that direction then about twenty yards further they found a bloody hand print on the pale bark of a Bilboa tree. Now they knew they were tracking someone who didn't care about leaving a trail.

As they followed the trail deeper into the forest it became apparent that this person had a destination they were trying to reach. Bill and Kelly continued following the trail for another two hundred yards when Kelly, who was in the lead, pulled up short, squatted down and signaled for Bill to join him. Bill moved up beside Kelly as quietly as possible. Kelly pointed at a large lump beside a tree about twenty yards ahead. Kelly signaled for Bill to move wide to their right while he would move straight in.

They moved towards the lump, as they moved closer they could tell that it was actually a man. What they couldn't tell was whether it was one of their guys or one of the enemy. When they got to within five yards they had not detected any movement, but that didn't mean that if it was an enemy he was faking. Kelly carefully moves forward to the side of the seemingly lifeless lump he is still unable to tell if it is one of theirs or an enemy. If it's an enemy soldier he's about to die. He reaches out and pokes the man with the barrel of his rifle. Slowly the man slumps further over on his side to reveal that it is in fact one of their own, the last man from team one.

Kelly steps closer to check the body, he gently presses against the man's neck to check for a pulse and is surprised to find a faint one. Kelly is completely surprised that they have found another member alive. He quickly signals for Bill to join him, when he does they lay the man on the ground and begin to assess his wounds.

"Bill he's still alive, but he's pretty beat up. Go get Dick and Mense tell them that we found Smitty. He' pretty beat up and we need to get him out of here." Kelly said as he tried to bandage what wounds he could. Bill started running up the hill crashing through the brush like a bull in a china shop. He made so much noise Kelly could follow his progress all the way to the edge of the tree line. Kelly smiled to himself as he listened to Bill go up the hill. 'That boy makes enough noise to wake the dead.' Kelly thought.

Bill reached the edge of the tree line and was able to gather more speed as he rushed towards Dick and Mense. When he got there he quickly explained what he and Kelly had found.

"We need to get him up here as fast as we can the chopper will be here soon." Dick said as they started back to where Bill had left Kelly. "Slick, stay here monitor the phone and keep tending to Gleason."

It only took a few minutes for Dick, Mense and Bill to get to Kelly and Smitty. Dick quickly unfolded the body bag and the three men quickly moved Smitty into it. They then picked it up and started carrying him to the improvised chopper pad. Just as they cleared the tree line they heard the chopper. They picked up their pace and arrived as the chopper was setting down. They didn't set Smitty down but rather placed him directly on the chopper. They then loaded the rest of the dead and wounded.

The dust-off took off and the team ran to retrieve their rucksacks before the next chopper set down to extract them out. They only had a few minutes to gather what they could and climb aboard. The chopper took off and again Kelly was amazed at the beauty of the mountains of Viet Nam. He had never seen mountains other than in pictures. He sat in the chopper admiring what he saw when the thought came to him that maybe someday when this war was over he could come back just to see some of the beauty this country had to offer. He still found it hard to believe that there was a war going on, the countryside seemed so quiet and peaceful.

They flew past small hamlets and slightly larger villages where, from the air, everything looked so quiet. He saw people out plowing fields with teams of water buffalos and mamma-sons doing laundry beside a small stream. They flew past a school and he could see the children outside playing. This just didn't live up to what he had seen in the movies. In the movies the buildings were not more than burned out shells and the people were on the verge of starvation. This just further confused Kelly. These seemingly pastoral scenes contradicted what he had been taught about the Viet Cong. He had been told that most Vietnamese held supporting views in favor of the Viet Cong and that simple fact made them an enemy.

Then there was the perception that the military wanted the soldier to believe, that there was an enemy behind every tree and he was just awaiting his chance to kill an American.

This went back to the very beginnings of warfare where commanders would use questionable tactics to de-humanize the enemy to such a point that the fighting soldier thought of the enemy more as an object than as a human being. This would make the soldier feel no guilt about killing his enemy and would do his very best to kill him before he himself was killed. Therefore, in earlier times there were such high body counts on the fields where the battles took place.

The chopper rides were usually relatively short no more than fifteen or twenty minutes. Almost always they are uneventful rides, but sometimes a chopper will be shot down or have a mechanical malfunction and will have to set down. When this happens it almost always involves the loss of life if the chopper is shot down. If it's a mechanical failure, the pilot is usually able to set the chopper down in an open area where the soldiers on-board set up a parameter and wait for the arrival of a replacement chopper. They are not alone because the pilot has radioed for cover support and there are gunships flying above them. Then the big Chinooks come in and lift out the crippled chopper and return it to base to be repaired. As for the soldiers, they are loaded onto another chopper and they continue with their mission.

During the chopper rides, it gives soldiers time to think about what awaits them or what they have already been through. Some of them causally glance out the doors at the passing scenery, some just sit there stoically, their faces not giving any clue about what is going through their minds. If they have just come from a battle, very little is said about what they just went through because it may mean having to admit to the loss of one of their own. This was something that soldiers didn't do. They didn't want to have to think that something could happen to them.

Kelly just sat looking out the door and wondering why they didn't bury the bodies of the enemy soldiers. He had always been taught that you treated the dead with respect and honored them. Coming to Southeast Asia he had to get used to a completely different way of thinking. Here the body was looked at as a transitionary object. Part of their religion was steeped in the theory of reincarnation. In that, if you lived a good life you would be reincarnated as a higher form. This was something Kelly didn't understand, the way he had been taught from early childhood was that when you die you either went to heaven or to hell. But he was too new in the unit to question any of the decisions of his superior officers or the men that had been in-country longer than he had.

Since this was something Kelly couldn't change, he decided not to think about it. He wouldn't think about all the carnage he had already seen, or the destruction war caused. He was still having trouble remembering that the enemy would show him no compassion, so he should also show none. He would become as hard as the men he was working with. When it came time for him to pull the trigger and end the life of another human being, he would do so with no remorse, because he knew that his enemy would not hesitate to pull the trigger on him. He could only hope that the decision to pull the trigger wouldn't make him loose his humanity; but he did know that it would change him forever.

It was also important that he form no lasting bonds with the men he worked with because they could be gone in an instant and he would be left with nothing but anger and pain. He would be friendly and join in the joking and teasing but he wouldn't allow himself to become entwined in their lives. The thought of losing them once he had become attached caused a lot of pain and pain was something he tried to avoid. But how could he not care? These were the men that his life depended on as much as they depended on him for theirs. This was quite a conundrum. It was almost a situation where you're damned if you do and you're damned if you don't. Either way he went there was pain involved. If he cared and they lost someone he faced the pain of losing them, where as if he acted like it didn't matter to him he would be isolated from the rest of the team. So how to solve this would take a lot of thought and self-reflection.

There was no time for thinking about that now since they were landing back at basecamp. After the chopper set down and the team had climbed off, they were greeted by Pete and a man Kelly had never met. He was dressed in civilian clothes and wore dark aviator sunglasses. This seemed odd to Kelly since he had not seen anyone that even had any civvies. The other team members seemed to know who he was but didn't bother with an introduction. Kelly got the distinct impression that no one on the team was even remotely happy to see this stranger. Pete told them to go put their gear away and then meet him in his office in an hour.

The team quietly made their way back to their hooch and put away their gear. No one said anything, they seemed to be lost in their thoughts and were only doing what was required to comply with the orders given them. The pallor of sadness that permeated the team was almost palatable. They had lost two teams in less than a week, they knew that there had to be a leak somewhere, but they couldn't figure out where. Finally, they gathered up the papers they had taken off the bodies of the enemy soldiers and headed for Pete's office. Maybe, after they were deciphered, they could get a clue as to where the leak was.

# CHAPTER 7

*Success is not final Failure is not fatal
It is the courage to continue that counts*

Sir Winston Churchill
(1874-1965)

Pete sat in his office quietly drinking a beer and discussing an upcoming mission with a man he had met with many times. This meeting was different because they were discussing a mission unlike any that had been attempted before. They were going to go into another country to kill an enemy soldier that had so far eluded them.

Jason Dobbs had been with the C.I.A. since its beginning. He had been in Korea during the war there and had been in military intelligence. One afternoon he had been summoned to his commander's office where he was introduced to a man named Harry Sizemore. Mr. Sizemore explained that there was a new intelligence unit being formed. He asked Dobbs if he would like to be a part of it. He replied that he would. From that day on Jason Dobbs had been involved in all kinds of covert operations. To him it was the thrill of being a spy that really attracted him to the "company".

"Do you think your boy can really do it?" Dobbs asked.

"Yeah, I'm very sure he can. He's one of the best we've ever had." Pete replied and took a sip from his beer. He was trying to size up the man sitting across from him.

"What makes you so sure he can do it?" the stranger asked.

"For one thing he was number one in his sniper class. Then there is his devotion to duty." Pete replied not liking the tone this man was using.

"I just wished we still had Jackson. That was a man I could rely on." The stranger stated.

Before Pete could reply there was a knock on his door and he shouted for them to come in. The team came in and stood together beside the door. They looked at the stranger and the air in the room suddenly became toxic. Kelly didn't know why but there was just something about the man that made him take an instant dislike to him.

"Gentlemen…." Pete said, "You all know special agent Dobbs. Probably not you Kelly, but Agent Dobbs is our contact at the C.I.A. He has come to ask for our help. It seems our old friend Major Tau has been up to his old tricks again. But this time we're going after him in Laos."

"Pete, before you begin; by international treaty we can't go into Laos. Has Dobbs explained how we are going to get around that one?" Dick asked. Dobbs rolled his eyes and shook his head.

"Dick, you let me worry about the treaties and stuff like that. You and your men just do your jobs. OK?" Dobbs said condescendingly. Pete could see this was about to get ugly and he didn't like Dobbs anyway; but he couldn't let one of his junior officers physically assault a C.I.A. operative.

"Look gentlemen…let's get to work and get this nasty business out of the way." Pete said. After a few grumbles and a promise that Dick was going to beat Dobbs' ass when this was over, they moved over to the map table.

After they had gathered around the map table Dick said, "Alright Dobbs, this is your party let's hear it." Dobbs then produced a couple of maps and some aerial photographs and spread them out on the table.

"Our sources have told us that Major Tau has become the area commander for a section of the Ho Chi Min trail running from the D.M.Z. (de-militarized zone) down to about Khe San. But he has made his headquarters over in Laos where he thinks we can't touch him. In private talks with the Laotian government they are willing to turn a blind eye to us going after him because they see him as a threat to their stability. In return they promise not to say anything if the North starts to create a stink." Dobbs explained as he looked around the table. "Furthermore, we have found out that he has been in contact with the Kamer Rouge down in Cambodia. This could bring about an entirely more complex set of problems if he goes through with what we think he's planning."

"So, you're saying that he is trying to carve out his own little kingdom." Dick said.

"Yeah, that's pretty much it. And we must stop him. He has already demonstrated that he is hardline against any western government. If he gets a foothold in this area it won't be long before we're fighting him and the Viet Cong.

"OK, so what's the plan?" Mense asked.

"I'm glad you asked," Dobbs said as he shuffled through the maps and photos. "This is a map of the area where his camp is, as you can see it is in a valley that is protected on all sides except for where the "trail" comes in and goes out." He said pointing to a valley on the map. "Our plan is to drop you guy's in about three klicks west of that valley and have you take up a position up here on the west side. Kelly what is the range on your rifle?"

"It's accurate up to about a thousand meters, why?" Kelly asked. "Can you get a good shot at that range?" Dobbs asked.

"If you're asking can I kill him at that range, the answer is yes." Kelly replied.

"Good, that'll work out just fine." Dobbs said.

"Wait a minute Dobbs," Dick said, "There is something going on here you're not telling us. Now what is it."

"OK…. OK, if you get caught the government will disavow any knowledge of your existence. This is strictly a covert operation." Dobbs explained.

"In other words, we have just become a hit squad for the C.I.A., right?" Dick said.

"That's one way of looking at it. But you could also think of it as a mission to save the lives of countless army and marine personnel. This guy, you'll agree, is dangerous and there is no other way to keep him in check except to kill him." Dobbs said. This got a nod of agreement from the team. "OK, now that we have that settled let's move on to the nuts and bolts of this operation."

"Here are some aerial photos of his compound. As you will notice there are two larger huts and seven smaller ones. We think that he is using the larger one on the left as his headquarters. From the topical map we think the best place for you to set up at is on this ridge, it's about five hundred meters from the target. Kelly, will you need any special sighting equipment?" Dobbs asked.

"No, just some non-reflective binoculars so I can get a good feel for his movements. I would also like a spotter." Kelly replied.

"You already have one." Dick said. "Who?" Kelly asked

"Me and there will be no discussion of it." Dick said decisively. "How fresh are these photos?" Mense asked.

"There're about two weeks old." Dobbs answered.

"I think we need some new intel from that camp." Mense said, "A lot can change in two weeks."

"You're right about that," Pete said, "What do you suggest?"

"Well…how about putting a small team in there? You know two or three men. Let them study the situation for two days and then get them out of there. That way we will have a fresh perspective of what's going on and whether he's really there." Mense replied.

"Who could we send? All the other teams are on missions or dead." Pete said.

"Well you could send me and Scuzzy Bill or Slick." Mense replied.

"Yeah, I could…but then if you get shot to hell who's going to cover these guys?" Pete said indicating Dick and Kelly.

"That's the whole idea boss, we won't get shot to hell." Slick said. "OK…You guys can go but we'll have you back here in two days. You'll leave in the morning." Pete conceded, "Is there anything else?"

"Yeah…I want to know everything you guys find out." Dobbs said.

"We'll give it to you in a report Dobbs." Pete replied, "Right now we just need to know the situation out there and to scout out a spot to watch from."

"OK but be sure to let me know if anything changes." Dobbs said authoritatively.

"Oh, you can be sure we will. But for right now Mr. Dobbs I need to have a word with my men. So, would you be so kind as to show yourself out." Pete said. Dobbs gave him a disapproving look and left the room.

After Dobbs had left Pete muttered a few curses under his breath. He had known him for a few years and still didn't like him. The man just seemed untrustworthy. Almost like he didn't tell someone the whole truth just the parts that would benefit him.

"Alright guys, here's how I see it. We go out check out this compound and see what's up. Slick, you and Bill can move in as close as you need to and get as good an idea of what's going on as possible. Confirm if you can that Tau is in fact there. Also get me some troop numbers that I can give to Dobbs to pacify him and keep him out of our hair for a while. In the meantime, Dick, you and Kelly study these aerials so you know that camp in the dark." Pete said. The team nodded their understanding and started to leave the room. "Gentlemen…Bumper has left to escort his cousin's body home. If you find any of his personal effects give them to Billy and he'll see that they're sent to him." Again, the team silently nodded and shuffled out the door.

The team silently walked back to their hooch, each man lost in his own thoughts. What was going through their heads was anybody's guess. When they reached the hooch, they all stopped in the doorway and looked at Bumper's bunk. The mattress was rolled up and the mosquito net was pulled closed. It was as if no one had ever been there. But they knew that someone had been there, and he had been a close friend.

"Where do you think he is now?" Slick quietly asked.

"Well, since he's only been gone a few hours my best guess is that he's probably down at Tan Son Nhut waiting for the flight home." Dick said wistfully.

"It's almost like he wasn't here." Scuzzy Bill observed quietly.

"But the good part is he's going home all in one piece and has lived to tell about it." Mense said.

"Yeah, that's true; but I wish he'd have gone home under different circumstance." Dick replied.

"But let's just remember that the good part about him going home is that we may get him back. Right Dick?" Kelly asked hopefully.

"No Kelly it doesn't work that way. Once he gets home he'll be re-assigned to a unit stateside to finish out his time." Dick explained.

"Then that means we'll never see him again?" Kelly asked.

"We might if we get assigned to the same outfit he's assigned to back in the world. But then again he may write and keep in touch." Dick said.

"It would be good to hear from him. Do you think he'll write Dick?" Scuzzy Bill asked.

"I hope so, Bill" Dick replied wistfully, "After all he was our friend." They all nodded agreement and Headed off to their own bunks. When they got there, they discovered that Billy, the company clerk, had delivered mail. Each one quickly got into the letters or packages that had been placed on their bunks. Suddenly Slick let out a loud yell and the team snapped to look in his direction. He was dancing around and hollering.

"Slick what is wrong with you?" Dick asked.

"I'm GOING TO BE A DADDY!!" Slick shouted. This brought cheers of congratulations and joking comments about the poor child; stuck with him as a father. It also brought friendly teasing back and forth amongst them. For a change they were able to celebrate something good, which lightened everyone's spirits.

"When did this happen Slick?" Dick asked.

"From what Denise says in her letter it happened the last night we were in Hawaii. That was some night let me tell you." Slick said with an evil smirk.

"Slick, you're a dirty old man." Mense called.

"No I'm not...I'm a sexy senior citizen in training." Slick replied laughing. This brought dissenting catcalls from the team.

"When is she due, Slick?" Kelly asked.

"She says here that her due date is the first part of April. She also says that there is a chance of twins since they run in her family." Slick stated.

"Oh, I hope she doesn't have twins; the world just isn't ready for more than one of you." Dick said.

The good-natured joking led to each of the team members telling how met his wife or girlfriend. Mense told how he had met his girlfriend Bonnie while he was doing some yardwork for her father. He explained that he and Bonnie had been dating for almost a month before her father found out. He told Mense that if he hurt her he would kick Mense's butt. He also related how he was scared to ask Bonnie's father for his permission to marry her. This brought a whole lot of advice from all corners; some of it was good advice and some of it were really bad ideas.

Kelly got a kick out of some of the stories and he started imagining what a life with Doris would have been like. Would they have had any children? What would he have done for a job? Would he continue to work on his father's ranch? Would Doris grow to be more attractive than she already was? Then the realization that these were things that he would never know because she decided that she wanted someone else came crashing in and the light and happy mood he had earlier faded like a puff of smoke in a breeze.

His blue mood continued through dinner and into the evening. Kelly was watching Mense and Scuzzy Bill getting their equipment ready for the upcoming mission when the door opened, and Lancer walked in.

"Hey Kelly, Billy left this over at our hooch by mistake." He said offering an envelope. Kelly took the envelope and looked at the return address. His eyes got wide and he couldn't believe what he was reading.... Doris Livingstone.

"Thanks Lancer, it's a letter from my girl." Kelly said as he quickly tore it open and began to read:

> *My Dearest Kelly;*
> *I received your letter the other day and I was shocked to say the least. First, my name isn't Kathie and second, I don't live in Seattle. Then I got to thinking about some of the stuff you said in the letter and realized that someone must have swapped envelopes on you. But no matter, I am writing to you to apologize for my last letter.*
>
> *I was felling lost and missing you terribly when Keith Salis started talking to me and started being friendly with me. I know there is no way I can make up for the pain I know I've caused but please try to forgive me. He caught me in a moment of weakness and I gave in to it. It's just that I miss you so much that I can't stand it. If you were here now I would smother you in kisses and never let you go.*
>
> *Well, it's almost time for the mailman to come and I don't want to miss him. Take good care of yourself and come back to me. I miss you so much.*
>
> *All My Love*
> *Doris*

Kelly reread the letter twice. Could he forgive her? Would he be afraid of her cheating on him again? Could he ever really trust her? These were things he had to think about but right now wasn't the time to linger on these questions. One big question he couldn't answer was if this letter would affect the way he did his job. The importance of his job had to take precedence over any personal matters for the time being.

But then, it did make him feel good to think that she still cared about him. Maybe there was still hope for them as a couple yet. Kelly started remembering what she looked like and some of the little quirks she had that he thought were so cute. Like the way she would always wipe her feet before getting into his truck. He once asked her why she did that and her reply was that she didn't want to be responsible for getting the truck dirty because he would make her clean it up.

"Hey Kelly, I don't know what you're thinking about but from that grin on your face it must be pretty good." Lancer said snickering.

"Just thinking about my girl." Was all Kelly said.

"Come on over here and look at this new piece of equipment H.Q. sent over, they want you to take it on the mission with you, so you can observe at night too. It's called a starlight scope." Lancer said.

"What's it do?" Slick asked.

"Well, it magnifies the ambient light from the stars and allows you to see in the dark. That way you can see at night without being seen. It doesn't put out any light because it has no light source. Let's go outside and try it out." Lancer explained. They all got up and walked outside.

"Lance, what do you know about this thing?" Dick asked.

"I was given a quick briefing on it, but I've never used one. My understanding is that you can see as well as if it were daylight." Lance replied. He then proceeded to explain what he had been told about the starlight scope and its operation. They then proceeded to put the batteries in it and turned it on. It made quiet squeal as it started up. When he looked through the eye-piece he let out an exclamation of surprise. He could see people walking around that he couldn't see with his naked eye.

"Man, this thing makes everything visible! I can see the hooches beyond the wire and everything." He exclaimed, "The only bad thing is that it's kind of heavy." Then everyone was clamoring to look through the scope. Finally, everyone had gotten a chance to look through the scope.

"Mense, do you think you could carry this thing with you on your little scouting trip" Dick asked.

"Actually, I was about to ask if we could take it along. We could get a good idea of what their night time routine was like." Mense replied.

"Good, go over to supply and draw a box of batteries to take with you." Dick said. "Hey Lance, thanks for bringing this thing over. It's going to make a big difference on this mission."

"No problem, since they've sidelined us until we get some replacements I couldn't see any sense in us just sitting on it." Lance replied, "By the way.... what is your mission?"

"As much as I would like to tell you I can't. Just let it suffice to say that we are going to eliminate a problem." Dick said, "That's all I can tell you. This is a top-secret mission, it's a need to know and right now you don't need to know."

"OK, OK I get the picture. But when this is all over you'll have to tell me about it. Deal?" Lance said.

"Deal." Dick replied as the two men shook hands.

# CHAPTER 8

*It is not your job to die for you country,
Your job is to make sure the
other guy dies for his.*

*General George S. Patton
(1885-1945)*

Kelly lay in his bunk when a soft sound from across the room peaked his attention. In the gloom he couldn't make out who it was or exactly where they were. As the sleep slowly left his vision and he became more acquainted with the dark he could make out someone sitting on the floor against the far back wall. He got out of his bunk and moved towards the figure. When he was within a few feet of them he recognized it as being Slick. He sat down beside him.

"What are you doing up, man? You've got a mission in the morning." Kelly said in a loud whisper.

"I know, but I don't know if I can do this anymore. I'm going to be a dad and I don't want to leave my child an orphan." Slick quietly sobbed.

"Man, you aren't going to leave anyone an orphan. You'll probably outlive us all. You've got to put that thought out of your head." Kelly replied. The two men continued to talk for another hour as Kelly tried to talk Slick back from the brink of despair. They talked about other more pleasant things until Kelly finally told him to talk to Dick in the morning and then he went back to bed.

Kelly climbed back into bed and lay awake just listening to the sounds around him and staring into the darkness. A slight breeze rustled the canvas roof of the hooch. He was amazed at how the darkness seemed to amplify the slightest sound. It was a sound that he had heard many times but never paid any attention to it. Now it seemed so loud that he was surprised that it hadn't woke up the entire team. But the rest of the team kept right on sleeping.

The hushed conversation he had with Slick seemed to have gone unnoticed by the team, but he had learned a lot about Slick that he hadn't known before. He learned that Slick had grown up in northeastern Chicago not far from the campus of Northwestern University. Slick's father had worked in an auto parts manufacturing plant and that his mother had been a secretary at a law firm.

Slick had explained that he learned early that hard work did have its own rewards. He had watched as his parent's careers had moved them ahead with regular pay increases and promotions. He had also learned the meaning of responsibility. When Slick was ten he had to walk his younger siblings to school and bring them home afterward. Then he had to take care of them until his parents got home. He had also learned that with the successful attention to his responsibilities there came rewards from unsuspected places.

An example of this was that when Slick got home with his two younger siblings he would use the time to do his homework and help the young ones with theirs. As a result, he became good at framing the concepts in such a way that they better understood what was being taught. He got so good at it that he began tutoring some of the younger kids in their neighborhood. This led to a letter of commendation from the P.T.A. and an offer of a part time job tutoring. His parents were very proud of him for doing that and thought that maybe he would someday become a teacher.

When his draft notice had come in the mail his parents were visibly shaken and disappointed. He had told them not to worry that when his military time was done he would return to Chicago and pick up where he had left off. But now that wouldn't be possible because he had seen and experienced too much of the darker side of humanity. The side he wished he could unsee and forget. But he knew all too well that was not possible.

Slowly sleep crept up on Kelly and the next thing he knew it was time to get up. He looked over at Slick's bunk and saw that it was empty, he then looked at Scuzzy Bill's and saw that it too was empty. He assumed that Slick had conquered his demons from last night. But then he saw that Mense's bunk was empty, that seemed strange since Mense liked to sleep in until the last moment.

"Hey Dick…. Where is everyone?" Kelly asked.

"Slick came to me this morning and told me about the conversation he had with you last night. He suggested that I send Mense in his place and I told him no I wouldn't; but what I did was add Mense to the team so that he would feel more covered. That seemed to satisfy him." Dick replied.

"You mean it's going to be just you and I on our part of the mission?" Kelly asked.

"No, it means that when they get back Mense will get some sleep and then we'll go and do what we have to do." Dick replied with a touch of exasperation in his voice. Kelly got the distinct feeling that Dick was not happy with him. "After we eat, go over to the armory and draw your rifle I want you to spend the day zeroing in at five hundred meters and seven hundred and fifty meters."

"Why so far?" Kelly asked.

"I've been looking at these aerials and the best place that looks like it could offer a clean shot is in this tree line to the southeast of the camp." Dick said pointing to a place on the map that was laid out on the table. Kelly looked at the map and then dug around in the drawer in the table until he came up with a ruler. He started measuring the distance between various points on the map.

"This figures out closer to four hundred than to five hundred." He said after a few minutes. "Figuring that I'll be shooting downhill, I won't have to worry about drop. I'll set the sight for a plus one and a half and go from there."

"Which rifle are you going to take?" Dick asked.

"I'll probably take the three oh three. That has a good range on it if we have to change locations." Kelly declared.

"Good choice why aren't you taking the H&H?" Dick asked.

"Well for one thing it doesn't have a collapsible stock and for another thing it's too heavy." Kelly replied.

"That makes sense, then I'm assuming that you're spending the day with the three oh three. Right?" Dick asked.

"Yep…. That's the plan anyway. Unless you have a better idea." Kelly quipped.

"No, that'll work out just fine. Now let's go get something to eat; I'm hungry." Dick said as he headed for the door with Kelly a step behind. They walked over to the mess tent and got their breakfast. They choose to sit at a table at the back of the mess hall where no one would bother them.

"Dick… you said that when I take that first shot it will change me, what did you mean by that?" Kelly asked.

"For one thing you will start viewing people and places as targets. You'll start seeing places as points of cover or shooters nests. You won't get the same enjoyment out of just observing the country around you. People will not have the same value to you that they did before. You'll start to see them as targets not as people." Dick explained.

"I'm sorry, Dick, but I can't agree with that. I look at this as a job and nothing more. If I must lose my feeling for humanity to do that, then I'm probably not very well suited for it." Kelly said.

"I didn't say you would lose your feeling for humanity, I said that you would start viewing people in a different way. You will stop seeing them as people but rather as targets. You won't have the same empathy for them that you would have for say a person with a terminal illness or very poor. You'll start viewing them as an enemy rather than a fellow soldier trying to do his job. Do you understand?" Dick said.

"Dick…. I've got to ask. Has this happened to you?" Kelly asked looking Dick straight in the eyes. Dick gently put his fork down and hung his head for a moment.

"Yes Kelly, I'm afraid that is exactly what has happened to me." He replied quietly, "I'm telling you this because you asked. I'm also telling you this because I know what it can do to you and your mind. If I see the signs that you're changing, I'll pull you out of the field and get you to a shrink, so you don't go crazy on me. Luckily for me Pete saw the signs and that's what he did for me. I think of you and the rest of the guys as my brothers and I'm going to do everything within my power to get you back to the world in one piece."

"But will I know the difference?" Kelly asked with a tone of confusion in his voice.

"You may. The one thing that you must watch out for is getting to like the job too much. You may be good at it, but you must always, and I do mean always remember they are people not just targets." Dick said looking intensely into Kelly's eyes.

"What do mean, liking the job too much?" Kelly asked.

"Well, do you remember the thrill you got in sniper school during the camo part when no one could find you?" Dick asked. Kelly nodded. "Well, it's something like that. You get to a point to where all you look forward to is your next mission; because you like the thrill of it. That's a dangerous way to think because you get to a point to where you think you're invincible and nothing can get to you or hurt you.

Then you're sent out on a mission and something goes wrong; someone gets hurt because you didn't use caution. When the mistake is pointed out and you realize that it was your mistake that got your buddy hurt, it starts eating you up inside. Before long, you become distant and don't want to be around people. You become hard and cold; because you don't want to feel the pain of knowing that a mistake on your part had cause someone else to suffer. But, at some time you're going to have to deal with the pain. It may take weeks, or it may take years. Do you understand?" Dick said intently.

Kelly looked into Dicks eyes and knew that he was telling the truth. Now Kelly had to wrestle with himself for control. Could he really become the kind of man that Dick had described? But the big question was not could he, but rather would he. Did he have the mental toughness to evade the pitfalls of his job? Kelly leaned back in his chair and just looked at Dick. The intense look on Dicks face told him that he was very serious about what he had said.

"Why are you telling me this now, just before my first mission?" Kelly asked.

"Because you asked, and I didn't think it would be fair to you to give you only half the truth." Dick replied, "Did that satisfy your curiosity?"

"I must say that you have given me a lot to think about." Kelly said quietly. "Don't think too hard it'll give you a headache. Just remember that you do have friends that care about you. We can't live your life but we're always going to be here to talk to. OK?" Dick said lightly. Kelly nodded.

"On to a more pleasant subject. What are you going to do about Doris?"

Dick asked.

"I don't know. I think I still love her, but I don't know if I trust her." Kelly said.

"I know what you mean, my wife and I went through something similar; but I was the one who cheated. It took me a long time to regain her trust. The best advice I can give you is to trust your gut. If you think you can forgive her for a moment of weakness, then by all means do so. But don't go have a fling just because she did. Two wrongs don't make a right. You know what I mean?" Dick said.

"Believe it or not I do understand what you mean. This is something else I'm going to have to think about before I write her back." Kelly replied.

"Good, you're approaching this like an adult, not a stupid kid. Now come on let's finish eating; we have a lot of work to do before the guys get back." Dick said.

The two men finished their meal in silence. Only as they were leaving the mess hall did either say anything. They had been lost in their thoughts about the subjects they had discussed. As they parted they merely waved, and each went in his own direction.

Kelly went to the armory and signed out his three oh three, his scope and a box of ammo. When the clerk asked him what he was going to do with all that ammunition he simply replied, "Sharpen up my skills," He then asked for directions to the long gun firing range. The clerk said he'd give him a ride since he had to go to the village to get the laundry.

After Kelly had been dropped off, he examined the range for a suitable target. The best he could do was an old jeep about five hundred meters out, he figured he could find something on the jeep he could put holes in. Then out of the corner of his eye he caught some movement. He quickly turned around to find Mr. Dobbs standing a short distance away.

"Come out to get some practice?" Dobbs asked.

"Yeah, I thought I'd blow a hole or two in something." Kelly replied coldly.

"Look Broadwick.... I don't much care what you think of me. Because to me you're expendable. I just want a job done. I've been tracking this bastard for six months and this is the first time we've gotten a clean shot at him. You understand?" Dobbs said with emphasis.

"Mr. Dobbs.... I understand that you want to get rid of Tau. But I really don't understand why you're coming at me like that. I haven't done anything to you, so what's your problem?" Kelly retorted.

"My problem is that they're handing this mission to a snot-nosed kid. I just wish Jackson was still here. Let me tell you, that man could shot. I saw him hit a quarter at a thousand meters." Dobbs said shaking his head with the memory.

"I'm better than Jackson. I beat his score in sniper school and I'll beat it here." Kelly said confidently.

"Yeah maybe, but this isn't school." Dobbs said and walked away leaving Kelly with the nagging feeling that he wasn't telling everything.

"Hey Dobbs," Kelly called after him, "What aren't you telling me that could be important to this mission?"

"Nothing.... not a single thing." Dobbs called back as he kept on walking. This bothered Kelly, since the inflection in his voice seemed to tell a different story. What could he be hiding from them? Did he have intel that could affect the mission? He figured he had better talk to Dick about this little encounter.

"You ready Kelly?" The range master asked.

"Yeah Serge, Hey, do you know that guy?" Kelly asked pointing his thumb at Dobbs who was now some distance away.

"Yeah I know him." The rangemaster said with a tone of disgust in his voice.

"Sounds to me like you're not all that fond of him." Kelly replied.

"I'm not. He's deceitful, and conniving. I wouldn't trust him as far as I could throw him." The rangemaster said.

"What makes you say that?" Kelly asked.

"Well…. I can't prove it, but, on every mission that he's been involved with the team that was on the mission got hit. I can't say that he's leaking information to the enemy, but it seems very suspicious to me." The range master explained.

"Yeah…. I see what you mean." Kelly said thoughtfully. "Can you get me a ride back to the compound? I need to talk to Dick and Pete."

"Sure, but aren't you going to get in a little target practice?" the range master asked.

"Later…. Right now, I need to talk to Dick and Pete." Kelly said.

# CHAPTER 9

*It's a terrible thing when someone you know
Becomes someone you knew.*

*Henry Rollins
(1961-?)*

"And you're sure of this?" Pete asked leaning back in his chair behind his desk.

"I don't know…. I'm only relating what Sargent Mallick told me out at the range. It just seems a bit strange to me that, if our guys are hit only on missions that Dobbs is involved with there might be reason for concern." Kelly replied.

"Mallick does have a point," Dick said, "What if Dobbs is the source of the leak? Wouldn't it be prudent for us to make changes in the mission that he wasn't made aware of?"

"That would be one way of either proving or disproving his theory. But if he is the source of the leak what do we do about it?" Pete asked, "We can't go to his superiors."

"No…. but we can take care of it ourselves." Kelly said angrily.

"Now, now…. we're getting ahead of ourselves. I will have a talk with General Kirkland and find out how he thinks we should proceed." Pete said, "He has the power to send him home if need be." Then turning to Kelly, "I'm not opposed to your idea either."

"Pete, there is just something about the guy that I don't trust, and this has just re-enforced that notion." Kelly said.

"OK.... I'll talk to General Kirkland this afternoon. In the meantime, get ready to go as soon as the bird touches down with the rest of the guys in the morning. Can you pack enough rations for them for three days?" Pete asked.

"Yeah.... We're only talking six extra meals. After we get into the field we can transfer them over." Dick said.

"But how are we going to get out of here without Dobbs finding out?" Kelly asked.

"The way I have it figured we're going to change the pick-up point on this end and then He'll be confused and will come to me for information. At that point I'll feed him some bogus intel and we'll proceed on with the mission." Pete replied.

"OK.... But where can we move it to that won't draw attention." Kelly asked.

"How about the dust-off pad at the aid station. There's choppers coming and going in there all the time. You guys can have Billy drop you over there before first light and I'll make sure the pilots know what's going on. One chopper in and out. Bill, Mense and Slick will not even get off the chopper; you guys will climb on the bird and away you go." Pete said.

"Not bad for spur of the moment planning." Dick said grinning.

The next few hours were spent discussing how to confirm that Dobbs was the leak and what to do about it. Pete placed a call to General Kirkland's office and requested a meeting; which he was granted. General Kirkland's aide asked what the meeting was for and Pete told him that it was a matter of security that needed immediate attention. Within a half hour of the phone call Pete was stepping from his jeep in front of the general's headquarters. He was immediately ushered into the general's office.

"Pete.... It's good to see you. How are things down at your end of the world?" General Kirkland asked.

"For the most part not to bad; but that's the reason I reason I came to talk to you, sir." Pete replied.

"James mentioned that you have a security problem." General Kirkland said, "Pete we've known each other for a long time, let's not stand on formalities."

"OK Bob, here it is. We suspect that a C.I.A. agent that we work with may be leaking operational plans." Pete said flatly, "Whether he's doing it knowingly or not we don't know."

The general just looked at him with no explosion on his face. Robert Kirkland had been in the army for almost twenty-five years and this was the first time he had ever heard such an allegation made. To his way of thinking the C.I.A. was a shadow organization that not many people knew what they did, except that they were a spy organization.

He had worked with several intelligence groups when he had been stationed in Germany. They mostly monitored the border between the NATO countries and the communist bloc. He had not heard of any of the details about what they really did. Most of the spying was done by people he had no contact with; he only got their reports.

"What makes you think that this agent is leaking information?" Bob asked. Then Pete laid out what they suspected and where they got their information. "That does sounds convincing, but it could all be coincidence. Have you taken any steps to limit his access to your operational plans?"

"Yes, we have." Pete said. He then went on to outline what the changes in the current operation were. General Kirkland sat quietly and listened to the changes Pete and the team had made.

"Do you think it will be enough?" Bob asked

"We hope so; we are changing the drop point and the general route they're taking. We also have a company of infantry on stand-by if we need them. They're just on this side of the border." Pete said.

"It sounds to me like you've got this problem covered, what do you need from me?" Bob asked.

"This part of the conversation is completely off the record, and just between you and I" Pete said.

"OK, but I don't see a reason for it." Bob replied.

"Bob if it turns out that Dobbs is the leak it's going to be hard to contain these guys. They're going to want revenge for his traitorous acts, they may go so far as to set him up and kill him. I just need to know that if that becomes a reality that my guys are covered." Pete said looking straight at Bob. Bob returned the stare.

"Pete, if your suspicions are right and Dobbs is playing both sides of the fence; you won't have to worry about your boys because I'll kill him myself." Bob said with emphasis and slammed his fist on to the desk. "If there is one thing I can't stand it's a traitor."

The two men continued to discuss the problem at hand and decided that Pete and the team were handling it the right way. Out of curiosity, if for no other reason, Bob asked how they would set him up to be killed. Pete said he wasn't sure yet but as soon as he found out he would tell him. This made Bob chuckle. Then Pete said, maybe a hunting accident, and then he laughed. Bob knowingly Nodded his head.

After Pete had left, General Robert Kirkland thought about what he had learned in his discussion with Pete and what he had suspected about the C.I.A. He had long suspected that they had a hidden agenda and were doing whatever it took to gain what they wanted. He had worked with them while he had been stationed in Germany and had found that the information they had given him was a very valuable tool. But now he was beginning to wonder, at what price did that information come? He was now questioning whether he should continue to put as much faith in their information as he had or whether he should just take it at face value and wait for field confirmation of it. He also wondered to himself if he should let his superiors in Washington know about Pete's suspicions. He then better of it since he didn't have any hard evidence. He figured that the people in Washington would figure he was crying wolf without any evidence. He would just have to wait and see what happens.

Meanwhile, Pete headed back to the compound with a renewed sense of being able to cover his men if need be. His discussion with Bob Kirkland had been very reassuring in that he didn't have to worry about covering up for his men.

When he arrived at the compound, he was greeted by the remaining members of team two. He knew that this was either a sign of bad news or they were anxious to hear what was said at the meeting. He was hoping more for the latter than the former. From the way they were standing he decided that it wasn't to deliver more bad news. Something he was truly grateful for, he didn't think he could take much more bad news.

"Well, what did he say Pete?" Dick asked.

"I told him about our suspicions and what we were doing about them. He said we were handling it correctly. He also said that if Dobbs is playing both sides of the fence he would take care of it himself." Pete said.

"Yeah… I'll believe that when I see it." Kelly snorted.

"I don't know Kelly, I've known Bob Kirkland for quite a few years and I've never known him to not protect his men. If he says he'll take care of it, I believe him." Pete shot back,

"No offence meant, but I've yet to see an officer that wasn't out to protect his hindquarters first." Kelly replied.

"No offense taken, but I guess we'll all just have to wait and see what happens. But, I don't think Bob Kirkland is anything like that, he came up through the ranks. He knows what it's like to have to pull K.P." Pete said.

"Pete…I just hope you're right." Kelly said with skepticism in his voice. Billy, the company clerk appeared in the door and called for Pete and the team to come into the orderly room. They all looked at one another in confusion and then followed Billy back into the orderly room.

"Slick, Mense, and Scuzzy Bill are headed in on a chopper." He said after they had all come in.

"How come they're coming back early? Did they say anything?" Pete asked.

"I didn't talk to them directly, but H.Q. commo called to advise me of their arrival." Billy explained.

"How long ago did they call?" Pete asked.

"About half an hour ago. Commo told me that they broke silence just long enough to ask for an extraction at thirteen hundred." Billy related.

"That can only mean that they either got detected or they have found out something that we need to know about immediately. If they were extracted at thirteen hundred," Pete said looking at his watch, "that would put them landing here any time now. Billy take the jeep and pick them up at the chopper pad." Pete said as he ran his fingers through his hair in a gesture of frustration. Billy nodded and headed off to pick up the rest of the guys.

"What do you think this means Pete?" Dick asked after Billy had left. "I don't know, but I'm thinking that it can't be good." Pete replied. "Has G-2 been monitoring their radio channels?" Kelly asked.

"Yeah, but they haven't heard anything but normal housekeeping traffic." Pete said.

"I wonder if their transmissions could be code for something." Kelly said. "Like what?" Pete asked looking at him questioningly.

"I don't know; maybe giving common object names to people." Kelly replied splaying his hands.

"Something like that would make sense, because that would not raise suspicion. It would just sound like what we would normally hear and would not cause anyone to be suspicious." Pete replied thoughtfully, "I'll have to call Major Harris over at G-2 and have one of his analysts look into it. Meanwhile, let's just wait and see what they have to say."

Pete, Dick, and Kelly continued to discuss what they thought could be happening. In what seemed like no time at all the jeep pulled up in front of the orderly room. The guys got out and came into the office as soon as their feet hit the ground. As soon as they had set their gear down they were bombarded with questions by Pete and Dick.

"What was so important that you decided to end the mission early?" Pete asked.

"We think we were compromised, shortly after we got there they started sending out patrols. From what we observed they knew we were in the area but not exactly where we were. We were able to dodge three patrols before things got too hot and we decided it was time for us to leave." Slick said.

"What makes you think they were looking for you?" Pete asked. "Well…the fact that all the patrols were concentrated on the west side of the compound. And that there seemed to be a briefing before each of the patrols went out." Slick replied.

"Uh-huh" Pete said thoughtfully, "What were you able to see before you bugged out?"

"We got the camp mapped out. They have built some cages out of bamboo and set them up towards the back of the camp. What they're going to be used for your guess is as good as mine." Mense said.

"How big were the cages? Are they big enough to hold a person do you think?" Dick asked.

"Yeah…. maybe. They had a small compound over on the east side that had a couple of pigs in it. We thought that to be a bit strange; it's the first time I've ever seen an army compound with its own farm." Slick replied, "We also observed several small trucks coming into the compound and parking in front of the main building."

"OK, let's look at the aerials and you can point out stuff. What did the cover look like?" Kelly asked.

"Well, for the most part it's forest but there is a ridge about three hundred meters out that has a good hedgerow that would offer good cover. That's where we set up." Slick said as he pointed to a spot on the map.

"Looking at these aerials I don't see any pig pens or any cages, so we know they're new. I don't see any reason for the pigs unless they're planning on being there a while and don't want to have to depend on their command for support." Dick said thoughtfully.

"Do you think we can get in and get the shot and get out with our hides intact?" Kelly asked.

"Yeah…I do." Slick replied, "But it will take a bit of luck. I mean, they're running patrols to the east like they were expecting something. What I was thinking was that we could move in on the west side where the patrols don't go and set up on the back side of the ridge, take the shot, and then bug out to the pick-up point."

"What were they using the small trucks for?" Dick asked.

"We couldn't tell they just came in, parked and then didn't move. We thought that was a bit strange. There is something about this camp that doesn't smell right." Scuzzy Bill said.

"Bill, while you guys were gone we think we may have found the source of the leak, but we have no proof. Now with you bringing back this intel and your gut feeling that something isn't right. Well, I think we need to keep our plans to ourselves." Pete said looking into the faces of the men around the table.

"Are you talking about going rogue?" Dick asked.

"NO.... not exactly. What I'm talking about is keeping Dobbs in the dark until our operation is over." Pete replied. The team all nodded in agreement.

"That's all well and good, but how are we going to keep him from finding out?" Dick asked.

"I'll call General Kirkland and have this declared top secret need to know only. That way he won't be able to sniff into what we're doing." Pete explained.

"When do we want to start this operation?" Dick asked.

"How long will it take you to get ready?" Pete asked. Dick looked at Kelly who just shrugged.

"About an hour, maybe a little more." Dick replied.

"OK...be at the chopper pad in three hours. In the meantime, I'll make the necessary calls and figure some way to send Dobbs off on a wild goose chase." Pete declared. The last part brought snickers from the team. They all loved the idea of Dobbs chasing his own tail, since none of them liked him. "OK, it's set then. Good luck and God bless."

The team quickly left Pete's office and headed out to do what they had to do to prepare for the mission. Slick and Scuzzy Bill headed off to supply to draw the rations; while Kelly and Dick again went over the maps and aerial photos. Slick went down to the armory to draw the ammo they would need. They returned to their hooch and began dividing up the weight so that each rucksack was pretty much equal in weight. Since Kelly had the added weight of his sniper rifle and the starlight scope, Dick distributed more of the ammo to the other men.

Dick looked at his watch, "It's time to go." He said plainly. The team struggled into their rucksacks and picked up their M-16s and moved out for the chopper pad. After about a five-minute walk they reached the pad and were greeted by a strange sendoff party. They were met by General Kirkland and several other high-ranking officers.

"Gentlemen, I've come to wish you happy hunting and to let you know that you don't have to worry about Dobbs. I had him put into solitary confinement until you get back." The general said, "I have left strict orders that he is to have no contact with anyone until I say so."

"Sir, with due respect, don't you think it's a bit of overkill to come down to see us off?" Dick asked.

"Maybe, but I didn't want him to color your decisions in the field and with him safely tucked away that will give you free rein." The general replied. Dick nodded with a wry smile.

"Sir, I would like to talk more but it's time for us to go." Dick said and then climbed on the chopper.

# CHAPTER 10

*Fear is created not by the world around us,
But in the mind,
By what we think is going to happen.*

*Elizabeth Gawain
(1948-?)*

The chopper ride was only about thirty minutes. But it gave Kelly a chance to look at the other team members and ask himself questions; such as 'will I be able to pull the trigger, or will I freeze? If I do pull the trigger, how much will it change me? Or, am I strong enough to do this. These questions were running through his head when Dick elbowed him in the ribs.

"Don't overthink this, it's just a job." Dick said just loud enough for Kelly, but no one else to hear. Kelly nodded and then started looking at the landscape as it flashed by. Soon the chopper pitched hard to the right and made a circle around a rice paddy, before it came in for a swift landing. The team was off the chopper in less than fifteen seconds and the chopper was airborne again.

Within minutes of exiting the chopper the team had disappeared into the dense foliage and began making their way to the site they had picked from the aerial photos. It took them what seemed to be an eternity to get there when in reality it only took five hours. When they finally reached a spot that offered sufficient cover they set their rucksacks down and began surveillance of the camp.

They were still baffled by the cages that had been constructed; what were they going to be used for? The mere size of them ruled out them being used to house animals. After they had been watching for about three hours they saw the reason for the cages. Slick was on watch with Kelly when they observed four men in ragged flight suites being marched in. They were marched up to the main hut and Major Tau stepped out on the porch, said something to the apparent man in charge and went back in. The four flyers were then marched over to the cages and forced inside.

Slick and Kelly looked at each other, Kelly signaled for them to fall back into the cover of the trees. They conferred for a moment then headed back to where the rest of the team was preparing for the rest of the mission.

"Dick, we found out what the cages are for. They just marched four flyers in and put them in the cages." Slick said, "From what we could see, they looked like navy flyers."

"What kind of shape were they in?" Dick asked.

"Their flight suits were pretty torn up, but for the most part they looked like they were in pretty good shape." Kelly said.

"Did they look like they could run if they had to?" Dick asked.

"I would have to say yes. Their clothes are torn, but I didn't see any blood." Kelly replied, "Why…. what are you thinking Dick?"

"Well, I'm thinking that we've seen a situation we can't ignore. If command tries to launch an all-out attack on the camp they'll kill the prisoners and disappear into the jungle. So, it's up to us to get them out." Dick said looking at each man, the looks on their faces told Dick that they agreed with him. "Here's my plan, Slick, you and I will sneak down after midnight take out whatever guards we need to; cut through the wire cut the back of the cages and lead them out."

"Dick that's a pretty good plan, but, that doesn't account for our original mission. I propose that like you said, you and I sneak down to the camp and get them out, but I also propose that Mense and Scuzzy Bill go along and provide cover for us if needed. Then at first light when Major Tau comes out Kelly takes his shot and beats feet out of here." Slick said laying out his plan.

"I see one major flaw in your plan, that is that it will leave Kelly totally unprotected." Dick replied.

"I can fend for myself, you guys get those fly boys out of there, so they can go home too." Kelly said defiantly.

"Now, now, don't go getting your panties in a bunch. Nobody is doubting that you can. I'm just saying that you are going to need a spotter and with Mense and Scuzzy Bill covering our butts that won't be possible." Dick explained.

"I've worked without a spotter before; so, I know I can do it. I can take the shot, spray the compound to add to the confusion and then beat feet for meeting place." Kelly stated.

"OK.... But if you should hear shots before first light spray the compound and bug out." Dick ordered.

"How will I know where you guys are?" Kelly asked.

"Well that's easy.... They're tracers are green and ours are red. Just shoot at the source of the green tracers." Dick chuckled. This brought a groan from the rest of the team. "I know it's not dark yet, but we should try to get some sleep while we can. I'll take the first watch, then Bill, then Mense, then Slick. Kelly we'll wake you up just before we leave."

"Ok" the team said in chorus. They then went about pulling out their sleeping gear and started picking their spots to sleep. They all chose an area under some low hanging branches that could hide them if necessary.

Kelly lay in his poncho liner just thinking about what was to come. He was going to be alone to make a critical shot. He won't have a spotter or someone to cover his butt if things go wrong. He'll be left to his own devises to try to get out and survive. He tried to recall the map and the terrain; and where they might meet up. These were the thoughts that were running through his mind as he drifted off to sleep.

Suddenly Kelly was back at the lake with his friends and his girlfriend, Doris. She was talking to everyone but him. He tried to talk to her, but she acted like he wasn't there. This seemed very strange to him, why wasn't anyone talking to him? He walked over to Doris and tried to grab her arm, but his hand passed right through it as if he were a ghost. Kelly didn't understand this at all. He was on a mission in Viet Nam so how could he be on a lakeside beach in east Texas. But how could he be in both places? As far as he knew he wasn't a time traveler, was he dreaming? That had to be the answer; it could be the only answer.

Then his best friend Jim Coleman said something about how it was a shame Kelly had died in the war. How could he be dead? He was on a mission. Then he saw a group of North Vietnamese marching onto the beach. He tried to yell for his friends to take cover, but nothing came out of his mouth. He watched as his friends turned towards the soldiers and were shot one by one. As each one of his friends fell one of the soldiers would laugh and point at him.

He awoke with a start and looked around. He was still in Viet Nam and still on the mission. This had all been a bad dream. He was breathing in short gasps, as if there wasn't enough air in the world to fill his lungs. Then he heard a loud whisper asking if he was all right. He replied that he was and then laid back down. The dream had really scared him. It was the first time he had ever had a dream like that. He wondered if this was the first of many or was it just an isolated case.

Kelly rolled up in his poncho liner and tried to go back to sleep, but the dream continued to haunt him. He just couldn't get it out of his mind. Was it perhaps a premonition, or could it be the product of an over-active imagination? Either way, it bothered him. He tried everything he could think of, but nothing could chase the dream away. Finally, he decided to set up for a while, maybe if he could find something else to occupy his mind the dream would go away.

When he sat up he noticed that it wasn't dark yet, so he moved over beside Mense, who was on watch. After a short discussion, he picked up the binoculars and went out to his sniper's nest. He thought if he could concentrate on the mission maybe, he could put the dream to rest. He crawled to the nest and began observing the camp.

Shortly after he began he saw four soldiers march a young girl into the camp and to the front of the largest hooch. They pushed her to the ground as Major Tau came out on the porch. Major Tau slowly stepped down to where the girl was lying on the ground. He was yelling at her, but Kelly couldn't understand what he was saying. Whatever he was accusing her of she was vehemently denying. He then yelled something at her and made a broad, quick hand gesture and the girl fell silent. Within the blink of an eye, he took out his pistol and shot her in the head. With a dismissive wave of his hand he indicated for the soldiers to dispose of the body. He then turned and walked back inside the hooch. After he had gone two of the soldiers grabbed the girl by the heels and dragged her outside of the gate to the edge of the jungle.

The actions of Major Tau shocked Kelly to his core. How could anyone have so little regard for a human life. What he had witnessed was nothing short of murder. This would not be tolerated in a civilized society. This may be a war zone but an act of pure barbarism such as this was intolerable. Kelly made a silent vow to himself that he would avenge this brutal assault on common decency.

He slowly crawled back to the encampment, when he got there he discovered that the rest of the team were awake. He was quickly bombarded with questions about the gunshot they had heard. Kelly quickly explained what he had seen and told Dick that he would gladly kill Major Tau. Dick replied that he had no doubt that he could. The meaning of what Kelly had said apparently was missed by Dick. But the vow Kelly had made to himself now carried more weight because he had told the team what he was going to do.

By the location of the sun Kelly could tell that it was about seven in the evening. He told Dick that he would stand watch for a while so that the rest of the team could get some sleep. Dick said OK and told Kelly to wake him at nine o'clock. Kelly agreed but said he didn't have a watch. Mense took his off and handed it to him with a comment that when they get back he should invest in one. This brought small chuckles from the rest of the team.

Kelly took the watch with a slight snort. He moved off to a point where he could watch the trail leading up to their encampment. After he had settled in he started thinking about what he was going to do after he got back to the world. The world was what the G.I.s call stateside because Viet Nam was an entirely different world than they were used to. As he sat concealed in the brush, he watched a mongoose sniffing around in search of a meal. When the animal caught his scent he quickly scampered away into the underbrush. Kelly lightly thought to himself that he didn't think that he smelled that bad.

Before long, it was time to wake Dick up. Kelly slowly and quietly made his way back to the small encampment. He tapped Dick on the bottom of his boot and he came instantly awake. Kelly gave Dick a brief rundown of what had happened over the last two hours, which was nothing, and then moved over and crawled into his own sleeping area. Kelly hadn't realized just how tired he was until he laid down. Almost instantly he was asleep and completely unaware of the watch changes until he felt the tapping on the bottom of his boot. He came instantly awake and in a loud whisper asked, 'what's wrong'. Dick replied that it was time for them to go.

"Here's the plan, we're going to go down to the camp and do what we have to do to get those flyboys out. I want you to go back to your sniper's nest and watch from there. If anything goes wrong and you hear any shooting, spray the camp with two magazines and then get the hell out of here. You remember that little stream we crossed about a klick southeast of here, that's where we'll meet up. If, when you get there, we're not already there, wait about an hour. If we don't show, you'll know that it all went wrong. You must make your way back as best as you can. Stay under cover and above all don't go into any villages." Dick explained.

"I understand, do you want the starlight?" Kelly asked.

"No, it'll be too cumbersome for us. You keep it here, you'll be able to watch our progress and you'll know if anything goes wrong. You'll also be able to direct your fire, if necessary." Dick replied.

"Here's hoping I don't." Kelly said. Dick just nodded. In the background he could hear the small soft sounds of the rest of the team preparing for departure. With instructions given the team moved out towards an undetermined location.

Kelly continued to sit in his sleeping place for several minutes after the team left, he was amazed at how even the smallest sound carried in the dark. He could hear the team moving when they were fifty feet away, after that there was nothing. This was when the realization that he was all alone sank in. The severity of the situation finally hit him; here he was in the middle of a dark jungle, surrounded by people who wanted to kill him and all he could think about was getting revenge for the young girl that he had seen so brutally murdered.

Revenge was an interesting motivator. No other human emotion could be as destructive to the psyche as the need for revenge. Whether the reason was real or only perceived didn't matter, the hate and lust was still there. Then when the slight had been avenged there was always the emotional letdown and the inevitable question, 'what do I do now?'. A question to which there is no stock answer.

Kelly finally got up and started packing his gear, he knew that when he took the shot there would be no time for him to pack up because whomever was second in command would be sending out people to find and kill him. He would have to be on the move almost immediately just to stay one step ahead of them. Once he was packed up he set everything he was going to need where he could grab it and go. He then began the tedious job of watching and waiting. About every five minutes or so he would turn on the starlight and scan the tree line around the camp to see if the operation had begun.

At what Kelly guessed to be about two he detected a small movement near the trees. He continued to watch as Dick and Slick stealthily moved out from the trees and into the cleared field. As they approached the wire a sentry rounded the corner of the fence, only to be immediately eliminated. One of the team cut the wire and the two men continued to move to the cages. That was when Kelly lost sight of them. A few minutes later he sighted a small group of men moving towards the fence. In mere seconds they were through the fence and moving towards the trees. When the last man had reached the trees, Kelly stopped watching because he knew that it was not time for him to do his job.

Kelly felt better now, his friends had been able to get into the camp and rescue the flyers and now all he could do was wait for the sun to come up and for Major Tau to make his appearance. While he waited in his sniper's nest he thought about Doris again. Being able to trust her was a big deal to him. Would she leave him for someone else again? Would she realize her mistake and try to make amends?

Sitting in the dark and thinking of Doris brought back lots of memories. Some were good, and some were bad. One of the best memories of her that he had was the night of their senior prom. They had been planning for weeks what they were going to wear and where they were going to go for dinner before the prom. He had wrangled a reservation at the Cattlemen's Club. It was one of the most exclusive restaurants in all east Texas.

Kelly had picked Doris up at about six in the evening and had been dazzled by the way she looked. She had decided to wear a very pale blue chiffon cocktail dress with a low-cut neck and a bare back. Her hair was done up in a big beau font hair style. To say that she was stunning was an understatement. They went to dinner and then to the prom. After the prom they decided to go out to the lake, so they could sit and "talk". When they got there Kelly produced a small bottle of whiskey he had bought through a friend. They broke the seal and took a small sip each.

"That wasn't half bad" Doris said smacking he lips, "As a matter of fact that tasted like another drink." She tilted the bottle and then handed it to Kelly, who also took a little larger drink. This kept up until the bottle was gone. They got out of the truck and walked down to the beach. The moon was up and cast a surprisingly large amount of light. In the moonlight Doris just casually walked through the sand barefooted since she had kicked off her shoes before they got out of the truck.

"What are you going to do after we graduate?" she asked.

"I don't know. Work for my dad on the ranch I suppose. I know I don't want to go to college. From what I've seen on the T.V., those guys with their long hair and all, aren't my cup of tea." Kelly replied distantly.

"But you need to go to college, Kelly. You and I both know that education is the key to everything." Doris said plaintively.

"But I don't want to go. It's too political and you know how I hate politics. Politicians are just a bunch of old guys who lie to get what they want and don't care about those of us that have to work for a living." He reiterated reaching for her. He pulled her close and kissed her deeply. He enjoyed kissing Doris because when he did she immediately reacted with an ardor that was hard to match.

"I must say, that's an appealing way to end a discussion." She giggled and started kissing him back. Doris was fully aware of where this was going to end up; both of them naked and having sex. But she wasn't opposed to it, for she rather enjoyed sex. Making love to Kelly was very pleasant, he was a very caring and gentle lover. She never failed to reach a climax with him.

Suddenly Kelly was jerked back to reality by a commotion down in the camp. He realized that the sun was almost ready to come up. He cursed himself for allowing his mind to wander away from his job. In the soft pale light, he was able to discern individuals through the binoculars. He observed two soldiers dragging the corpse of the guard back into the center of the camp. Kelly decided now was the time, so he picked up his rifle and sighted down into the camp. He searched through the scope to try to find his target. Finally, he found Major Tau standing on the front porch of the largest hooch.

"Now it's your turn to pay for all of your deeds." Kelly said quietly to himself as he lined the crosshairs on Major Tau's left ear. Kelly slowly applied pressure to the trigger. The rifle suddenly jumped as the round exploded on its way. In a micro-second Major Tau's head exploded, sending blood and brains all over the porch and his second in command, who had been standing beside him.

The suddenness of the fatal attack left the captain stunned and immobile. Kelly ejected the spent round and lined up on the captain, who was still apparently in a state of shock just looking at the carnage. Kelly once again squeezed off another round which found it's mark in the center of the captain's forehead. The impact sent the back of the captain's head all over the porch to join that of Major Tau's.

Now the remainder of the gathered force were looking in all directions trying to find the sniper. A few dove for cover, but for the most part they all stood motionless not knowing what to do. Kelly picked up his M-16 and began spraying the gathered group with fire. When he had used up his two clips he quickly crawled back to where he had stashed his gear. He quickly packed his sniper rifle, put a fresh clip into his M-16, got on his rucksack and began to run down the backside of the ridge.

He didn't wait to see what kind of damage he had done to the camp. He knew he had put a serious dent in their command structure. But, he also knew that there would be others to take Major Tau's place. They could only hope that the new commander is not as bad as Major Tau was.

After Kelly had run about two hundred yards down the trail he stopped to catch his breath. As he stood listening he could hear shouts at a distance, he didn't think they would find his nest that quickly. He thought he would have more time to make good his escape. He began to walk towards the stream crossing where he was to meet Dick and the rest of the team. As he went he could hear the enemy soldiers coming. He decided to set up some booby-traps to slow them down.

He carefully set two hand grenades with concealed tripwires about one hundred feet apart. Then he continued on his way down the trail, next he found a spiderweb across the trail and set another hand grenade with a trip wire concealed as part of the web. Kelly figured this would definitely slow them down. An air burst like that does a lot of damage for about fifty feet. After encountering three booby traps in less than three hundred meters they will be very careful, which will really slow down the pursuit. They will have realized that their unknown sniper is as good at evading capture as they are. As a result, they will become more careful and as a result will give Kelly more time to rejoin the team.

When he had gone about two hundred meters he heard the first booby trap go off. He smiled an evil smile just to think of their surprise. He turned toward the sound of the explosion and gave them the one finger salute and then hurried off down the trail thinking, "That'll teach you."

# CHAPTER 11

*Real difficulties can be overcome, it is only
The imaginary ones that are unconquerable.*

Theodore N. Vail
(1845-1920)

After hearing the explosion of the booby trap Kelly moved with haste but at the same time caution. When he had gone about three hundred yards he heard the second one go off. This time he actually laughed out loud and thought to himself, "You boys are in for a long afternoon."

He knew he was coming close to the stream crossing when something caught his eye. The grass had been trampled in an apparent rush to get off the trail. He knelt to study it better when a voice called to him in a loud whisper. He stood bolt upright and looked around. Then suddenly Dick popped up out of the grass. Kelly relaxed his stance.

"BANG, YOU'RE DEAD!" Dick called to him and then smiled broadly. "Yeah maybe, but I wouldn't put it to the test if I were you." Kelly retorted. Then they both laughed. Kelly moved towards Dick's position as the latter got up off the ground.

"Well…. Tell me, how'd it go?" Dick asked.

"I put it this way…. Major Tau will never kill anyone again, but then neither will his captain." Kelly said.

"You mean you got them both?" Dick asked with shock in his voice. "That's exactly what I'm saying." Kelly replied.

"We heard the two shots and then the spraying of the camp. But what were those two explosions?" Dick asked.

"Oh, nothing much… just a couple of hand grenade booby traps I set to slow them down." Kelly chuckled.

"Damn…. You're a nasty little bastard aren't you." Dick said laughing.

"Hey, if they can do it to us, why can't we do it to them? This is a guerrilla war isn't it?" Kelly asked.

"You do have a point." Dick replied nodding his head, "Come meet our guests."

They Walked another hundred yards back into the dense foliage to a small clearing next to the stream. There he saw the rest of the team and four very bedraggled pilots. "Gentlemen, this is Kelly Broadwick, he's the one we've been waiting for." Dick said making a sweeping gesture with his hand. As each one was introduced they shook hands. "How far behind you are they?" Dick asked.

"My best guess is about a mile or so." Kelly replied as he slumped down on the ground.

"OK, then we better get to stepping, it won't take them long to cover that." Dick said.

"Oh, they're going to be slowed down at just any time now." Kelly said. Just as Kelly spoke the third booby trap was tripped, he started laughing almost hysterically. Everyone started looking at him like he had lost his mind. "That's the third one. I set it up in a tree. I have no doubt they are really getting scared about now. Having their own tactic turned around on them is no fun."

"Damn Kelly, remind me not to piss you off." Scuzzy Bill said

"OK, let's get going before they recover. Slick you take point." Dick said. The nine men started off with Slick walking point, then came Dick and Scuzzy Bill, then the four pilots, and then Mense and Kelly at the rear.

They walked at as quick a pace as the pilots could tolerate. Apparently, from what they had told Dick, they had been captured individually and brought to a holding area just north of the camp. Then about a week ago they started being marched day and night to the camp they had just been freed from. The pilots didn't speak Vietnamese, but one of their captors spoke pretty good English. They found out that he had been educated in the states and then went back to Viet Nam. He had told them that they were going to be transferred to Hanoi and held as prisoners of war.

After they had walked for about an hour dick called a halt for a rest break.

They moved off the trail into a dense thicket of bamboo. There they set a guard and rested for about twenty minutes, Mense had passed his canteen to Kelly since his was empty. While they had waited for Kelly, the team had filled their canteens and rested as best they could. Their pace was further slowed because the pilots were wearing sandals, the North Vietnamese soldiers had taken their boots and then laughed when their feet bleed while walking to the camp.

Dick was about to call for the choppers when Slick came back to where they were and quietly announced he had spotted a North Vietnamese patrol headed their way. Slick stated that they had just come over the ridge and were moving quickly. He said there were about six or seven of them.

"Dick, do we have any claymores?" Kelly asked.

"Yeah, I think we have six. What are you thinking? Setting up some more Bobby traps?" Dick asked.

"Sort of…. You get these guys to the chopper and I'll keep the dinks off your back." Kelly replied.

"Kelly as your commanding officer, I can't allow you to do that. Secondly, as your friend I can't allow you to do that." Dick replied

"Look Dick…. We don't have time to discuss this. Just give me the claymores and any ammo you can spare. I'll be alright…. I promise. And when I get back you'll buy the beer." Kelly replied. Without waiting for a reply Kelly started loading up the explosives into his rucksack. Dick shook his head and moved over to help.

"You know you're one crazy son of a bitch, don't you?" Dick said. "Yeah…. It might have to do with being kicked in the head by too many horses back in Texas." Kelly replied with a grin.

"OK, look, here's the map we'll give you three days to get back across the border then we're coming after you. The green beret camp is here," Dick said pointing to a spot on the map, "Right now you're only about twenty klicks from the border When you get to the border there is a crossing station right here. Have them call command and we'll send a bird to you immediately. Got it?"

"Yeah, I got it, but you guys better get going or we're all going to be in this fight." Kelly said as he hoisted his rucksack to his back and started back up the trail.

He had a plan, but he hadn't quite worked out the details. His basic plan was to distract the patrol and head them off in a different direction away from the team and the pilots. After he knew that they were safely away he would then concentrate on getting himself out. The first part would be fairly easy; but the second part would be more difficult because he would have to double back through enemy territory. That could be a little dicey.

As Kelly moved back up the trail to where he had seen a small branch trail going off, his mind was going a thousand miles a minute calculating where to set up his ambush. If these guys could ambush American troops why couldn't he give them a taste of their own medicine?

When he reached the branch trail, he headed back up it for about twenty yards, then he moved off the trail into a bamboo thicket. He climbed into a nearby tree, so he could get a better look at the area. When he had found what he was looking for he climbed back down and dug two claymores from his rucksack and went about setting up his ambush. He set the claymores about twenty feet apart one on each side of the trail. Since there were only six or seven of them he might be able to wipe out the entire patrol in one hit.

After he had set the mines and hidden the wires, he moved back into the brush where he couldn't be seen and waited for the patrol. As he sat behind the bush he thought just how pretty South Viet Nam and Laos really were. It was too bad that he had to see it through the eyes of someone fighting for their life. He thought that if he got out of this alive maybe someday he could come back and tour the country. That would be ironic, coming back to the place where he had committed a state sanctioned murder. But then, maybe there won't be problems since this is a war.

Suddenly he heard a twig snap. The time had come to start the show. Kelly began to intently watch the trail; waiting for the patrol to make their appearance. He didn't have to wait very long. He saw them walking out of the tree line about a hundred meters from the trap. "Come on, keep coming.", he thought to himself. Then within seconds they were all with in the kill zone. He lowered his head and compressed the two plungers at the same time.

The roar of the explosives going off was deafening. This was quickly followed by men screaming. He raised his head slightly to look through the vail of dust to assess the damage. He couldn't see anyone standing, but he did see several bodies that looked like they had just been put through a meat grinder. One of the bodies had no face and another was missing an arm. All around the bodies there was huge chunks of flesh and pools of blood. He was able to count six bodies. That could mean that either he got them all or one of them got away. He decided to go back up the trail from where they had come to check for any sign of a blood trail. Kelly decided to leave his gear hidden in the thicket until he got back. He moved out of the thicket slowly and quietly. He approached the bodies but didn't see any movement. He moved past them and started slowly scanning the ground for traces of anyone moving back up the trail. After he had gone about fifty yards and found no sign, he figured he should get back to his gear and start his long walk back to the pick-up point.

When he reached his gear, he took out the map that Dick had given him and started plotting his next move. Faintly he could hear choppers. "Well, I did my job. I bought you guys enough time to get the flyboys out, now I've got to get myself out." He thought.

After examining the map for a few minutes, he put on his rucksack, picked up his M-16 and started walking east towards the border. As he passed the bodies littering the side of the trail he looked into the dead eyes of one of the soldiers and a shiver ran down his back.

"By the grace of God, there lie I." He said and then continued walking.

He had wrought a terrible toll on the enemy, but then that was his job. What was it General George Patton had said, *'It is not your job to die for your country, it your job to be sure the other guy dies for his.'* Kelly had always liked that quote. He thought it summed up the job of a soldier very well. As he walked, he would periodically stop and confirm his location. During this time, he would also listen for any sound that could indicate pursuit. He could not believe that another patrol hadn't been sent out to find out what had happened to the one he had destroyed. Whenever he would see a farmer working in the fields he would detour into the trees so as not to be seen. That evening, just a little short of dark he made his way up into the hills in search of a place to bed down for the night.

As he was climbing he saw what looked like a hole in the ground. He went over to investigate. What he found was the entrance to a cave. Kelly set his rucksack down and found his flashlight in one of the side pockets. He shone the light through the entrance and was surprised to see there were no inhabitants. He expected to see a rat or a mouse, but he didn't see any of that. Nor did he get the strong ammonia smell of bat guano. The cave entrance was large enough for him to squeeze in and then drag his rucksack after him.

Once inside he was surprised at the size of the chamber. It went back at least forty feet and was about fifteen feet wide. As he neared the back the ceiling continued to rise from about five feet to about fifteen feet. Kelly shone his light around and saw that there were no side tunnels leading off the main chamber.

Once he had made his inspection of the cave and confirmed that he was the only living thing in it, he unpacked his poncho and poncho liner and prepared to go to bed. It had been a long day and he could use some sleep. Since he was in a cave he didn't think it would be necessary to put out sentry traps. These were tin cans with pebbles in them strung from a trip wire. The noise of the pebbles in the can would alert him to someone being around when they shouldn't be. He got out his evening meal ate it and then bedded down for some well-deserved rest.

Kelly thought about how he would wake up, he didn't have a watch to set the alarm. After some consideration he just went to sleep and figured he would wake up when he woke up. Sometime during the night, he had the urge to go to the bathroom. When they were in the field he would just step off the side of the trail and let fly, but in his cave, he didn't want to smell it all night. He got up and went back to the entrance, listened for a few minutes then crawled out and took care of business.

As he stood peeing he looked up at the sky and was amazed at the number of stars he could see. He didn't remember seeing that many back in Texas. Kelly thought it was a beautiful sight and he just wished Doris could see it. But then, if she were here he probably wouldn't be doing the job he was doing. He crawled back into his cave and went back to sleep.

Out of nowhere, Kelly found himself again on the lakeside beach in East Texas. He found this quite strange, he was the only one on the beach, but he could hear his friends talking. What they were saying made no sense to him, they were just jumbled up words with no clear meaning. Kelly felt very confused, he couldn't see anyone, but he could hear them. Then suddenly he was awake. He didn't hear anything, but it was light outside, he could see the light coming through the entrance he had crawled through.

After sitting on his bed for a few moments he decided to go look outside to see what he could. He could tell by the softness of the light that it was very early. Kelly moved over to the entrance and slowly poked his head out. From his vantage point close to the ground he couldn't see a lot, but he could see that the valley was shrouded in ground fog, which was typical for this time of year. In the distance he heard a water buffalo mooing. It reminded him of early mornings on the ranch back home. This brought a twinge of homesickness.

Kelly decided it was safe for him to venture out of the cave and continue his trek. Then he noticed the footprints in the dew on the grass. Someone had been there. They weren't large prints, but they were definitely human. They looked like those of a small child. What would a child be doing out in the hills this time of day? Kelly moved further out of the cave but couldn't see any more foot prints. He thought that this was very strange. He climbed back down into the cave to retrieve his gear and rifle, when he came back to the surface there was a small woman standing a short distance away. She was dressed in faded black loose pants and a faded black top, she also wore a flat conical hat that he had seen almost all the farmers wear. She looked at Kelly and put her finger to her lips in the quiet sign. Then she indicated for him to follow her. Kelly was reluctant to go off with someone he didn't know but she was unarmed, and he was.

She led him towards the direction he was going to be going anyway, so this seemed to be good so far. When they got to the top of the ridge she again motioned for him to be quiet. Then she pointed towards the trail he would have taken, below and to the right he caught a glimpse of movement. Then he saw six soldiers appear from the brush. She motioned for him to follow her and they started down the side of the hill they had just climbed up. When they were close to where he had first discovered her, she indicated for him to get down. They watched as another patrol passed by about one hundred meters downhill from them.

"Who are you?" he whispered when the patrol had left.

"I am called Mai Ling Fong, I'm Chinese but I don't believe in what my government is doing." She explained, "I want to go to the United States. I have family there, but I don't have the money to travel with. If I help you escape the way I did then maybe you can put me in touch with the right people, so I can go to the states."

"You speak pretty good English; how do I know this isn't a trick to get me captured?" Kelly asked skeptically.

"Right now, I can only give you my word that I am who I say I am. The only way for me to prove to you that I'm not lying is to lead you to the American Army camp at LO Bok Lin. When we get there, I will turn myself in and you can speak for me." Mai said timidly. Kelly thought about this for a moment.

"How far is it to the camp?" Kelly asked already knowing how far it was. "About a day's walk if we start now, but we will have to be careful; there are North Vietnamese patrols everywhere. Word has been sent out that you murdered Major Tau and Captain Diem. Then you blew up the patrol sent out to find you. Is that true?" she asked.

"Yes Mai, it's true. Except, that it wasn't anymore murder than what I saw him do to a young girl day before yesterday." Kelly replied, "She was unarmed and begging for her life when he shot her in the head and had two soldiers drag her body out into the jungle to be eaten by the creatures there." Mai made no reply, she just shook her head.

"He was a bad man, he ruled this area with a tight fist. It's a good thing you killed him." Mai finally said, "We better go before they come back."

"You're right we should go, but that doesn't tell me why it is that you speak such good English." Kelly said.

"My family in the United States told me that the better I spoke the language the easier it would be for me to enter the country. I learned English from a teacher of mine in school. He thought that I wanted to be an interpreter." She explained. This all made perfect sense to Kelly, but he wasn't going to trust her completely until they got to the American camp.

"OK, I have to trust you for now. Let's go." Kelly said after thinking for a few minutes. They started walking in the same direction that the patrol had taken, but they stayed in the trees. When they had to cross a valley, they would do it at its narrowest point to limit their chance of being seen. After they had walked for about for about four hours they stopped to rest. Kelly asked how she knew he was in the cave, she explained that she had stayed there the night before and had seen him go in.

Off in the distance they heard the sound of a chopper, this was a good sign to Kelly that his trek was almost over. Something had been bothering Kelly and now he felt he had to ask. Why hadn't they gone to the border station? Her reply was simple, it was run by men Major Tau had put there. He would have been shot on sight. Again, this made perfect sense to Kelly, so he accepted her explanation. But something just didn't seem right, but Kelly couldn't put his finger on it. He just hoped he would be able to figure it out before it was too late.

While they were stopped Kelly had been looking at his map. From what he could tell they would be to the Green Beret camp before dark. Then he thought, why didn't she go to an American camp, explain her situation and ask for help? And why would she be living off the land out in the middle of nowhere. She didn't just happen on him by chance, she had been waiting for him. The only thing he could figure was that she was a plant.

"Mai, I want you to tell me the truth, why are you helping me?" Kelly asked.

"So that you will speak for me with your superiors." She replied innocently.

"I don't believe you Mai. Too many things just don't add up, like where you knew to find me. Secondly how did you know who I was. And thirdly, there are too many holes in your story. She just looked at him, but he could see the change in her eyes and he knew he was right.

From out of nowhere, Mai produced a knife and charged at him with a primal scream. Having been trained in hand to hand combat Kelly was able to disarm her quite quickly. But she continued to kick and scream at him. After fending off her anger filled attack, he finally grabbed her by the arm and was able to subdue her. He laid her on the ground and kneeled on top of her. He reached into his rucksack and pulled out a short length of parachute cord. He grabbed her wrists and bound them together. Then he sat her down at the edge of the clearing a few steps from his rucksack. She continued to cry deep racking sobs in anger and kicked her feet in frustration.

"OK now, who are you really?" Kelly asked.

"I am Mai Nguyen of the People's Army of North Viet Nam. One of the men you killed was my husband, Captain Van Nguyen. I vowed to find you and kill you myself." She spat at him through her tears.

"And when did you plan to kill me?" Kelly asked.

"When we got to the American compound. I was going to stab you right as we passed through the gate and then run off into the jungle." She sniffled.

"Well honey.... your plan obviously isn't going to work. I must give you credit you did play the part very well. You had me fooled until I got to thinking about your story and found too many holes in it. Now get up it's time to go." Kelly said with a slight snarl. Kelly helped her to her feet and started down the trail behind her. He wasn't about to let this she-devil out of his sight. After they had walked for about two hours she said she had to go to the bathroom, so would he please untie her hands.

"Not on your life, I'll pull your pants down and hold them, so you don't pee on them." Kelly said with a chuckle. To think she could talk him into untying her hands, she must be crazy.

Kelly did as he had promised and didn't do anything more. After all, losing her husband and then getting captured trying to avenge him, he figured that was enough of an insult from him. When she was finished, he pulled up her pants and they started down the trail again. When they had been walking about an hour Kelly suddenly stopped. Grabbed Mai and ducked into the thick undergrowth.

While they lay there, Kelly kept his hand over Mia's mouth to keep her silent until he could determine if the sound he had heard was friendly or not. After a few minutes he saw a small column of men approaching. When they got closer he recognized the green beret one was wearing. Kelly carefully stood up with his hands away from his body. When they sighted him, they pointed their weapons at him until he spoke.

"Wait…. don't shoot. I'm American." He said loudly. Almost instantly they lowered their weapons and started at him at a brisk walk.

"Are you Kelly Broadwick?" the soldier that seemed to be in charge asked. "Yes I am." Kelly replied.

"We were told that you would be coming. I'm Captain Greg Lasiter Fifth Special Forces Group." The leader said offering his hand. "By the way good hunting, we've been trying to get rid of Tau for a long time. Who do we have here?"

"This is Mai Nguyan, wife of Captain Van Nguyan, deceased. She led me through the jungle and tried to kill me because I killed her husband." Kelly explained.

"Very good, we have a place for her. Come on let's go we're only about a half mile from the camp." Captain Lasiter said as he turned and headed back down the trail. One of the men checked the bonds on Mai's wrists then pushed her ahead of him. Kelly fell in right behind the Captain. In what seemed to be no time at all the camp came into view.

# CHAPTER 12

*You will never be the person you can be*
*If pressure, tension and discipline*
*are taken Out of your life.*

*Dr. Janes G. Bilkey*

When the chopper set down Kelly was surprised at the size of the welcoming committee. There was Dick and the team, Pete and a tall man Kelly had never seen before. He thought for a moment that he could be in some serious trouble if all these people came to pick him up. He got off the chopper and approached the group.

"You didn't have to set up a welcoming committee for me." Kelly said to Dick.

"Trust me this isn't a welcoming committee." Dick replied shortly.

"If it's not then what the hell is going on?" Kelly asked now sure that he was in some serious trouble.

"Kelly, you have done something we have been trying to do for months. Then on top of that you bring back a prisoner, a very valuable one at that. She is going to be a wealth of intel for us. But disobeying a direct order is something we can't afford in a close group like ours." Pete said. Kelly felt his heart sink, he knew this would be the end of his career.

"It worked out good this time, but if you do anything like this again I'm going to hang your hide from the yardarm. Do you understand me?" Pete said in a stern voice. Kelly could feel his heart rise a bit, maybe he wasn't going to get court martialed after all.

"Yes sir." Kelly announced loudly.

"But you are getting a silver star for bravery." The stranger said. Kelly looked at him in disbelief; that was when Kelly noticed the two gold stars on the man's collar. Then he looked at the rest of the party and they were smiling. The joke had been on him. Then everyone gathered in close to shake his hand and congratulate him.

"By the way Kelly, allow me to introduce General Edward Collier, commander of the special operations group." Pete said. The general extended his hand and Kelly shook it.

"Pete let's go to your office to finish this discussion. It's getting too hot out here for my taste." General Collier said. This was greeted with nods and comments of agreement. Pete and the team climbed into one jeep and the general got into his. In no time at all they were in the cool confines of Pete's office.

When everyone had settled in and gotten a beer, Pete and the general began asking Kelly questions about what he had seen. Kelly quickly and concisely answered their questions. When asked about Mai Nguyan, he was a bit more tight lipped. He didn't want to tell they that she almost killed him. If he had been a bit slower, he would probably have a knife in his chest. But what he did tell them was that he observed a lot of activity in the valleys, there were quite a few N.V.A. patrols along the border. He further described how Major Tau had arranged for his people to be put into positions of power at the border crossings. Kelly also stated that Mai had indicated that something big was coming, but she didn't say what it was. She only said that the streets would run red with the blood of the American dogs. This caused General Collier to sit back in his chair and scratch his head.

"She didn't say anything about what it might be, right?" General Collier asked.

"No sir, she just said that there would be no safe place for the American dogs that have invaded her country." Kelly replied. Then before the general could ask any more questions there was a knock on the door.

"Come in" Pete called out. The door immediately opened, and a young officer accompanied by Billy the company clerk came in.

"Did you get it Harry?" the general asked the young officer.

"Yes sir." Harry replied patting his briefcase. The general smiled, glanced at Pete and the other members of the team. They all nodded.

"Sargent Broadwick, front and center." The general called out. Without hesitation Kelly stood up, stepped in front of the general and stood at attention. "It is with the greatest of pleasure that I award you the permanent rank of First Lieutenant for meritorious service above and beyond call of duty." The general then pinned a silver bar onto Kelly's collar.

"Lieutenant Van Meter, front and center." The general called after pinning the bar on Kelly's collar. Dick set his beer down and stepped in front of the general with a confused look on his face. "Lieutenant you have exhibited exceptional leadership and decorum. It is with equal pleasure that I am honored to promote you to the permanent rank of Captain effective immediately. Congratulations." Dick had a look of shock on his face as the general removed the single bar and replaced it with the twin gold bars.

The general stepped back and saluted both men and received a textbook salute in return. The general then called,

"Dismissed" the team and Pete rushed the two men and began pumping their hands in congratulations. It seemed like everyone was talking at once.

"Lieutenant Broadwick, as your first duty as a commissioned officer why don't you buy us all a drink over at the club." Pete called out above the din. Kelly nodded and laughed. How he got this he didn't understand, all he did was what he thought was best for the mission. He was able to buy time for Dick and the team to get the four flyboys safely away.

"ATTENTION" Kelly call out and everyone snapped to attention and the room went silent. "My first order is that we all adjourn from here and reconvene at the club for drinks. That is if the general doesn't mind."

"I don't mind at all Kelly." The general replied with a light chuckle. "Would the general care to join us." Kelly asked.

"It would be my pleasure. But before we go allow me to get rid of some of this hardware on my shoulders. Sometimes it makes people nervous to know that there is a general in the house." The general replied. With that he removed the two stars from his collar and followed the rest of the team over to the club. True to tradition, Kelly bought the first round of drinks. When they were gone Dick bought the next round. This continued for the rest of the evening. Eventually someone brought up Dobbs. The general said for them not to worry about him, he had arranged an assignment that would have him chasing his own tail for a long time.

While the group was walking over to the club the general made it clear that they were not to call him general, but instead to call him Ed. He said that he wanted that for the same reason that he took off his stars. Everyone agreed, and the evening was set. Along about seven o'clock Kelly asked Ed had any ideas for dinner. Ed told Harry to hunt up his cook and have him prepare steaks for the just whole group. This was greeted by cheers from the whole group.

"Ed it's been a long time since this crew has had a good steak. May I take this opportunity to say thank you on behalf of us all." Pete said with a slight slur from drinking all afternoon.

"Well, let me say it's been a long time since I have been able to be one of the boys. An officer of my rank is supposed to maintain a certain decorum. But you guys have allowed me to let my hair down, and I thank you. If there is ever anything I can do for you just say the word and I'll do everything I can." Ed replied. This brought a round of cheers from assembled group. "Now let's go eat some steaks."

The idea of good food brought the team and Pete to their feet immediately. They all gathered around Ed and sang 'for he's a jolly good fellow' all the way over to the general's private mess. When they got there the cook had already started baking potatoes and fixing salads. They took their seats around a table that had already been set for them. Just as they got seated Clarence, the cook, appeared and took their orders just like in a restaurant. After the orders had been taken they started talking about general topics, when someone noticed that there was an empty seat. That's when Ed noticed it as well.

"Harry.... Why are you standing by the door?" Ed called out.

"I wasn't invited to this party, sir." Harry replied in a stiff voice. "Soldier.... you have two seconds to put your butt in this empty chair or I'll have you on K.P. for the rest of your life. Now get over here and sit down. You make me nervous standing by the door." Ed called back to him. With a sheepish grin Harry immediately joined the fun and was warmly welcomed.

Pete had been sitting and watching the comradery unfold. But something had been bothering him, why was Ed there at all? He understood that Kelly had made the invite to join them all for a drink, but why had he come to the compound at all? Was something going on that he hadn't picked up on?

"Say Ed…. Could I have a private word with you?" Pete finally asked. "Sure, let's step outside." Ed replied. They both got up and walked outside.

"What's on your mind Pete?"

"Well…it just seems strange to me that you would show up when you did. You've always given me a heads up that you were coming and don't tell me that you were just in the neighborhood. What's going on?" Pete asked.

"Ok Pete, we've known each other too long for me to try to snooker you. I came down to size up your guys for a very special mission and I wanted to see what they were like." Ed replied in way of explanation.

"What kind of special mission?" Pete said.

"Well, without going into details, I can tell you that there are some very large risks involved and I wanted to meet your guys personally to be sure they could handle it." Ed said in a loud whisper.

"Look Ed, my guys are about as good as your going to find. They know their jobs and they do them very well. I would be willing to put them up against any outfit there is and know that they would come out on top." Pete replied vehemently.

"Pete you don't have to convince me. As far as I'm concerned, they are the best. Now just a brief overview, this mission is going into Northern Laos and bringing back a body, alive if possible. It's a project that Dobbs started. Right now, I can't give you any more than that." Ed said.

"In other words, it's a snatch mission that could mean their lives if they get caught, right?" Pete said quietly, "And this is like the banquet they gave the gladiators before they fought in the arena."

"That's a bit extreme, but yes, it is." Ed replied, "Look this last mission proved your guys can think and plan on the fly. There may be a bunch of that on this mission. It's already been turned down by those glory hounds over in special forces, your guys are the only ones left who might have a chance of pulling it off."

"Will they have any kind of support?" Pete asked.

"They get all the support we can send them. But there seems to be a build up around Khe Son and we don't know what's going on. Your guys are going after the only man that can tell us what's going to happen." Ed explained. Pete's eyes got wide.

"You want my guys to kidnap General Van Cho!" Pete said excitedly, "You're out of your mind! He's surrounded by an entire division of highly trained North Vietnamese regulars. That's the Red Tiger Division, they are the best of the best."

"Yes, I know all that, but we have a spy in there and the good general is going to be taking a vacation at Tam Lo Loc. That's when we'll move on him because he will only have his personal guard with him." Ed said quietly.

"How will we know when he goes? It's not like they make an announcement. What is the timetable for this operation?" Pete asked.

"We're looking at a start of possibly tomorrow I won't know until after I hear from our spy." Ed said, "Whatever you do don't say anything to anyone about this. This is strictly top secret."

"Can I let the guys in on it?" Pete countered.

"You can, but make sure that they know they can't say a word to anyone. With this being one of Dobbs' operations, I want to be sure we have all of the facts and figures." Ed reiterated.

"OK I won't say anything to them until in the morning." Pete replied with a sigh, "We better be getting back inside, those guys may have eaten our steaks by this time."

"Well, if they did it's not a problem; I have more. That's one of the advantages of being a general, I eat good." Ed said with a chuckle as he slapped Pete on the back.

# CHAPTER 13

*"It is all to do with the training;
You can do a lot if you're properly trained.*

*Queen Elizabeth II
(1926-?)*

The sun had risen fully into the sky and there had been no movement from the team four hooch. Everyone knew that the team was back from their last mission and had heard of the heroics that Kelly had pulled off. They also heard about the promotions of Kelly and Dick. Most everyone had heard them come back from the club last night, to say that they had been a bit loud was an understatement. But no complaints were made because everyone understood how infrequently good things happen in a war zone. They accepted the loud behavior as some men just letting off steam.

Pete, on the other hand, was suffering from a nasty hangover because he joined team for back at the club after they had left General Collier's private mess. It seemed that each time Billy would type something on the typewriter, Pete's head would pound. He had to admit to himself that he couldn't drink like he used to. Did this mean that he was getting old? Probably not, just that he was out of practice. But then, there hadn't been too much to celebrate lately.

He got to thinking about what Ed Collier had told him last night about the up-coming mission. He had known Ed Collier since their days at Fort Benning. Ed was a young captain back then trying to make a good name for himself. Some people thought that he was a bit brash, but everything he turned his hand to seemed to work out. But Pete wasn't so sure about this one. He had never known him to sugar coat anything and for that matter he usually went to the darker side of the situation. Maybe that's the case this time, but that is something only time will tell.

"Billy.... Have you heard or seen anything of Dick and team four?" Pete called out.

"No sir, I haven't heard a peep out of them. You want me to go down there and roust them out?" Billy called back.

"Yeah, why don't you. we shouldn't be the only ones suffering this morning." Pete said with a small chuckle, "Tell them I need to see them as soon as they can get here."

"Will do, boss." Billy replied and headed out the door letting the screen door slam shut. That bang was like someone drove a spike through Pete's already aching head. Pete made a silent vow that he wasn't going to drink like that ever again, then he took two more aspirin and another cup of black coffee.

Billy was walking down what passed for a street towards the team four hooch when he saw Dick coming out of the latrine. Dick looked very disheveled and hungover. Dick saw Billy coming and put his finger to his lips signaling for him to be quiet. Billy started snickering to himself, these guys really tied one on last night, he thought.

"Hey Dick, Pete wants to see the whole team in his office as soon as you guys can get there." Billy said quietly.

"OK, tell him we're on our way.... Slowly, but we're coming. By the way, thanks for not yelling, I think my head would explode if you did." Dick replied equally as quietly.

"Man, you guys really went after it last night. But it was fun." Billy said a bit more loudly.

"Billy if you keep screaming like that I'm going to kill you myself." Dick snarled. This was more than Billy could take, he burst out laughing. This didn't help Dick's hangover or his state of mind. "I swear Billy, I'm going to kill you." Once again Billy started laughing as he turned and headed back to the orderly room at a fast trot. Dick watched him go and thought 'I'm never going to do this again.'

Dick turned and returned to the hooch, when he was inside he loudly said, "Alright ladies hit the deck we got business to do." This was greeted by a chorus of groans and catcalls referencing Dick's parentage. There are also a few comments about what he could do with any business he needed to do. But, in short order they all got out of bed and began to get dressed. As they were getting dressed, more than one of them swore they would never do this again. Dick thought to himself, 'yeah, not until the next time.'

"Alright guys, Pete wants us all in his office as soon as we can get there. So, let's get cracking." Dick said.

"Man, those railroad tracks have already gone to your head." Scuzzy Bill said.

"Bill, one more crack like that and I'll show how they have gone to my head." Dick replied. This brought a chorus of oh-h-h's from the rest of the team and a sheepish grin from Scuzzy Bill.

"A bit touchy this morning aren't we." Slick snickered.

"Yes, I am, because someone couldn't quit buying drinks." Dick retorted as he looked at each one.

"But you must admit, we ate good.... I think. It's all a blur did we get drunk last night?" Mense asked. This started an entirely new conversation about what had transpired the evening before.

"Hey guys, did you notice how quiet Pete got after him and Ed went outside?" Kelly asked to no one in particular.

"Now that you mention it, I did notice that he became kind of reserved. But, we were having so much fun I didn't think anything of it." Dick replied contemplatively.

"Maybe it had to do with you guys getting the promotions." Slick said. "Yeah, maybe, but I doubt it. I think there's more to it, I think he knows something, and he didn't want to tell us about it." Dick said, "Oh well, we'll find out soon enough. Let's go see what he wants."

With that Dick started for the door with the rest of the team following in a straggling fashion. As they walked up the street towards the orderly room, they continued to speculate about the change in Pete's demeanor the previous evening. The speculation ran from Pete wanting to retire to him having some incurable disease. This was contributed by Scuzzy Bill and got calls of disgust from the team. They soon reached the orderly room and walked in.

"He's on the phone right now with General Collier. He said for you guys to wait and he'll be with you as soon as he gets off the phone." Billy told them. The team settled into the chairs scattered along the wall, a couple of them picked up magazines and started thumbing through them. The rest of the team just sat with their heads resting against the wall and their eyes closed. Billy had no doubt that their heads were still pounding from the night before, he was glad that he had ducked out when he did.

After about fifteen minutes, Pete came out and motioned for them to come into his office. He told Billy that if anyone wanted to see him tell them to come back later. Also, to hold all his calls except for a call from General Collier. He was to put that one through immediately. He also said that he was expecting a package from General Collier and to bring it to him as soon as it got here. Billy said he would do it.

When Pete returned to his office after giving Billy his instructions, he motioned for the team to take a seat. "Gentlemen, we have a problem. There seems to be a buildup of enemy troops across the border from Khe Son and nobody knows what's going on. There is only one man that knows the answer to that question and he's over in Laos. General Collier wants us to go get him." Pete explained.

"With due respect to the general, but isn't that against the law for us to go into another country like that?" Dick asked.

"Technically, yes. But from what I've been told it's pretty much the same situation as what we had with Major Tau. But with this mission we're going to bring back a person and turn him over to the C.I.A. Is everybody with me on this so far?" Pete asked. The team all nodded their understanding.

Suddenly there was a light rapping on the door followed by Billy appearing and entering. He walked over to Pete and handed him a large manila envelope. "I believe you were looking for this." Pete said thanks and Billy quietly eased out of the room. Pete then ripped the envelope open and took out the contents. He started handing smaller envelopes to the team. They looked at them with a mixture of curiosity and confusion. He indicated that they should open the envelopes.

Inside each one was a picture of a North Vietnamese General and a map. The map was of the area around Tam Lo Loc, an area known as a resort of sorts for the North Vietnamese command staff. Some of them brought their families there to spend time with them others brought their concubines, indentured women used for sex, just for a little release from the tensions of command.

The picture was of General Van Cho, who was reputed to be Ho Chi Minh's top advisor. To bring him back alive to be interrogated would be quite the prize. There were other aerial photos of the compound that showed the general layout and the location of the security emplacements. The compound seemed to be well protected, judging from the photos.

"Pete, if I'm reading this correctly, command wants us to go in and kidnap Van Cho and bring him back. Is that it?" Dick asked.

"Yeah, pretty much." Pete replied nonchalantly.

"Man, they really don't want much do they?" Slick said sarcastically.

"I know this is a lot to ask of you guys, but command seems to think that we are the only unit that can do it. Personally…. I would rather have told them to go to hell, but, I'm not in a position to do that." Pete replied.

"Whose crackpot idea was this anyhow?" Scuzzy Bill asked.

"Well…. If really must know…. it was a project Dobbs was working on before he was reassigned to whatever it is he's doing now." Pete told him. This revelation brought moans and groans from all members of the team.

"Pete, you know as well as we all do that anything Dobbs is involved in is never what it seems to be. Look at what he just sent us out on. We brought back four flyers that we didn't even know existed until we got there. And then on top of that it almost cost Kelly his life. I just don't trust that little bastard." Bill said with a tone of finality.

"I'm in agreement with you on that, Bill. I don't trust him either, but this came down from command and we're obligated to try to carry it out." Pete replied, "You guys know that you can call no joy at any time during the mission if it looks like you can't get it done."

"Pete how did General Collier find out about this mission?" Kelly asked. "Well from what I understand, Dobbs went to General Collier with it about two weeks ago. I also understand that right now there are elements of the Seventy-fifth Rangers doing a scout mission on the camp and we should be hearing from them at any time. They're supposed to be back sometime today." Pete related. Just as Pete finished speaking, the phone that linked him directly to command rang.

After a short call Pete said, "Alright boys lets go."

"Where are we going?" Dick asked.

"To H.Q., the rangers are back, and General Collier wants us there immediately." Pete replied. Without hesitation the entire group headed off to command headquarters. On his way out, Pete told Billy where they were going and that he wasn't sure when they would be back. Billy just said OK.

When they pulled up in front of headquarters, they were met by the young officer that they had met the night before. He shook hands all around and said for them to follow him. He led them deep inside the command bunker passed numerous rooms with squawking radios. Then they came to a door that looked as ominous as it could be with an armed guard beside it. The guard opened the door and the team entered. The door was closed loudly behind them. This sent chills up Kelly's back. "This can't be good' he thought.

The team found themselves in a large room with just a table in the middle and a single light above it. There were several men around the table looking at some maps, all conversation stopped, and the men around the table looked at the team with no expression on their faces.

"AH, team four, welcome gentlemen." General Collier said. The team moved forward and shook hands with the rangers as they were introduced. There was some small talk between team four and the rangers as they had worked together on other operations and were familiar with each other.

"Alright gentlemen let's get down to business." General Collier said.

"OK general." Captain Craig of the rangers said. They spent the next two hours going over every detail of the camp at Tam Lo Loc. They referenced the aerial photos so that everyone knew which building was being talked about. After a short meal break they then spent the biggest part of the evening going over the terrain and possible escape routes. They also were briefed on the location and timing of the security patrols. Since Tam Lo Loc wasn't a military base there was no barbed wire. But the rangers did point out that there were roving patrols.

While the rangers were there no sign of General Van Cho was seen. But, what they did see were four lines of defense. The first and second lines were out away from the main part of the compound and could easily be penetrated or by-passed. The third was a loose roving patrol consisting of four men walking in opposite directions, two walking clockwise around the compound and two walking counter clockwise. The fourth line was a tight group set at gun emplacements at each corner of the building. This last line would be the hardest to by-pass since they were always manned. To get past this line could take some real planning and execution of the plan. One small mistake would mean being captured or worse, killed.

The idea was brought up that some kind of diversion could be done to drag the guards away from the corners of the building. But no one could come up with an idea of how this could be done, they had ruled out any kind of air assault because there weren't supposed to be any American troops in Laos. It might be possible that some of the local tribes' people could help, but that was discarded because no one spoke their language. It was finally decided that an all-out simultaneous assault on the four emplacements would be the best. It was left up to team four to figure out the details when they were on site. This didn't thrill any of the members of team four, but it seemed to be the best plan available.

The meeting then adjourned, the team was given the photos of the compound to study and memorize. They needed to know that compound well enough that they could walk it in their sleep. Even with this in-depth discussion of the mission, Kelly got a bad feeling about this one. He felt that there was just too much that could go wrong. But then if any of it went wrong, the whole mission would fall apart.

The plan they had decided on had Kelly picking off the guards in the corner emplacements from a hilltop about a quarter of a mile away. From the hilltop he would have a clean shot at three of the four emplacements. To add to the confusion, he would use a silencer. That way the enemy troops wouldn't know where the shots were coming from.

In the briefing, they discussed whether to do this at night or during the day. It was decided that Kelly would shoot at night and use the starlight scope. He said he would need time to sight in the rifle with the scope. Everyone agreed that if the timing of the mission would allow it, he would go out to the range at night and sight it in. He said that he would need a silencer, so he could check the rebound of the night scope to the muzzle flash. This everyone agreed to. General Collier said that he would have several of them sent over immediately.

The meeting adjourned, and the team climbed into their jeep and headed back to their compound. During the ride no one spoke they were all lost in their own thoughts. Kelly was thinking about Doris and the dream he had. He couldn't understand what brought it on. He knew he cared a great deal about her, but he wasn't sure what she really thought about him, and that's where his indecision sprang from. He was wondering if he could write to one of his friends and have them check up on her.

They arrived back to the compound and headed back to their hooch. As they walked, they talked aimlessly about anything that came to their minds. This was just a device to keep from thinking about what might happen on the next mission or the one after that or the one after that. They knew that on some mission one or maybe all of them were going to be killed or wounded. That was just something they preferred not to think about.

The best way to keep from thinking about it was to talk about more pleasant subjects. Kelly asked the question, "If you think you love someone, but you don't really trust her; what do you do?" This stopped the whole team dead in their tracks. They all looked at him and thought for a moment.

"Kelly, my young friend, the best advice I can give you is that there are a lot of fish in the sea. If you lose one, well you just bait your hook and try to catch the next one." Scuzzy Bill said putting his arm around Kelly's shoulders. The team looked at Bill like he had lost his mind.

"No man, that isn't the way to go about it. You have to find a way to test if she is really committed to you. I mean, after all, just because she says she loves you doesn't make it so. She could just be playing you for what she can get." Slick added. This began an argument that the whole team took part in. One side saying yes, that was the thing to do and the other saying no it wasn't.

Suddenly the air was cut with a very high-pitched whistle. Everyone turned to see the source. Who they saw was Pete. With his hands on his hips shaking his head.

"You guys sound like a bunch of old women fighting over who has the best apple pie recipe." He said then he turned to Kelly, "Son, if the good lord wants you two together then he will find a way to make it happen. You just have to trust that he will make it happen. But remember, it'll be in his time not yours."

"But Pete, all I think about is should I trust her to be faithful." Kelly said in a plaintiff voice.

"That's OK Kelly, if it's right he'll give you a sign. Now…. Enough about your love life. We just got the call that our target is going to be leaving Hanoi day after tomorrow for the retreat. That means that we must be ready as soon as we get confirmation that he's there. Kelly, can you be ready with only one night's practice with the scope?" Pete said.

"Yeah…. I think so. I'll go as soon as the silencers get here." Kelly replied. "Well, you won't have to wait long because they got here about ten minutes ago." Pete chuckled.

"OK then, I guess I'll go tonight." Kelly said, "Who wants to spot for me down range?" Nobody moved to volunteer.

"Alright…. if you're not going to volunteer, Bill you're on the spotter scope and Mense you're on the target down range." Pete said with a tone of finality. Since Pete was the unit commander, his orders were law. The men accepted their assignments with just the smallest of grumbles. "Kelly check in with Sargent Rockwell and get the operating manual for them. I want you to be able to put them together in your sleep."

"Yes sir." Was all Kelly said and then headed over to the supply shed where the armorer, Sargent Rockwell, had his office. The armorer looked up when Kelly walked in.

"Man, you got here quick, I didn't think you'd be coming over until tonight." He said as he stood up.

"Well, Pete told me to come and get the manual for the silencers and know it inside and out. Also let me have one of them so I can see the parts in real life." Kelly replied.

"I'll do you one better," the armorer said as he placed a box about a foot square on the counter, "here's the whole shipment."

"How many are in there?" Kelly asked. "I think there's fifty." He replied.

"The general must think I'm going to do a lot of shooting sending me this many." Kelly chuckled.

"Well, knowing what these are going on and what they are used for; I'm just glad I'm not the one on the receiving end." The armorer countered with a slight nod of his head.

"Thanks, I'll remember that." Kelly replied gathering up the box and heading out the door.

He made his way back to the team hooch and entered just in time to hear Slick declare that women were the scourge of men everywhere. This started a philosophic discussion that Kelly was only half listening to. Injected into the conversation were the common jokes about not being able to trust a creature that bleeds for seven days yet doesn't die.

"Hey Kelly, what do you think?" Slick asked. "About what?" Kelly replied.

"About women." Slick said.

"Well…. The way I look at it is that man struggles for nine months to get out then he spends the rest of his life trying to get back in." Kelly replied with a straight face. This brought hoots of laughter from the rest of the team.

"Kelly that's the smartest thing I think I have ever heard you say." Dick said around his laughter, "What's in the box?"

"It's the silencers and the operating manual. I need to read up on these things. I've never used one." He replied. The rest of the team got up and moved over to get a closer look at the new equipment as Kelly pulled one from the box.

It didn't seem to be a complicated piece of equipment, but it's proper use would have deadly consequences. It appeared to be a matt black cylinder about six inches long and about an inch and a half around. The armorer had already taken the sight off the end of Kelly's rifle and replaced it with the screw on fitting for the silencer. Kelly began reading the manual while the rest of the team took turns looking at the silencer.

"According to the manual, this thing is good for about ten shots then it has to be replaced. It muffles the sound of the shot and eliminates the muzzle flash completely. It says here that no sound will be heard ten feet away. But it doesn't say anything about what it does to the accuracy." Kelly read.

"I guess that's what we're going to find out at the range tonight." Scuzzy Bill said looking at the tube.

"Yeah, tonight." Mense snorted.

"Hey Dick, is Pete going to give us another guy since there is only five of us?" Kelly asked.

"He hasn't said anything. But with a mission like this he wouldn't just pop someone new on us, I do know that." Dick replied, "By the way do you want bull's eye targets or silhouettes?"

"I would prefer silhouettes, that way I can get the sighting down to within a half inch." Kelly replied matter of factly.

"Good call." Dick said with a nod of his head.

# CHAPTER 14

*In our constant search for security we can never
Gain any peace of mind until we
are secure in our own souls.*

Margaret Chase Smith (1897-1995)

After the sun went down team four made their way to the firing range. They were able to get the rifle sighted and locked in. This took just a little over an hour and a half. The team then went back to their hooch and went to bed. They had an exciting two days, with Dick and Kelly getting promoted and the ill-conceived celebration afterwards. Then Pete dropping the bombshell of a mission on them, and now a late-night rifle practice. It was no wonder that they all went to bed as soon as they got back to the hooch.

For once the team got an entire night's sleep. When they awoke the next morning, they were rested and all signs of the hangovers of the previous day were gone. They went to the mess hall and got breakfast then went back to their hooch to study the materials that General Collins had sent over. They studied the maps and tried to locate a good drop off point as well as a good pick up point. Both points had to be in South Viet Nam because of international agreements. Laos was a no-fly zone as far as American choppers were concerned.

The best that they could come up with was a high mountain meadow about a klick and a half east of the border.

With this information in hand Dick went to see Pete and let him know what they had come up with. Dick wasn't happy about having to hike almost thirty miles to reach their target but with the restrictions placed on them it could have been worse. He strolled into the orderly room and told Billy that he needed to see Pete.

"Pete's not here." Billy said.

"When will he be back?" Dick asked.

"I don't know, he got a call from General Collier and ran out of here like his ass was on fire. He didn't say where he was going or when he would be back." Billy related. Dick stood and thought for a moment.

"When he gets back give him these coordinates, they are the drop off and pick up points we were able to come up with. If he has any questions, come and get me. OK?" Dick said.

"Not a problem. Hey Dick, while you're here you want the mail for your team? I'll save me a trip." Billy said.

"Sure" Dick said accepting the two boxes and small bundle of letters. But before he could leave a jeep came to a sliding halt outside stirring up as much dust as anyone could imagine.

Pete rushed through the door and headed straight for his office. As he went he told Billy to go down and get team four and tell them to get to his office immediately. Billy just pointed at Dick, who was standing on the other side of the door.

"That was quick Billy! I'm impressed."

Pete chuckled, "Come on in Dick."

"What's up Pete? You flew in here like the devil himself was after you."

Dick replied.

"Well, in a way he is. Van Cho left a day early and he is due to arrive at the compound this afternoon." Pete related.

But how does that effect our timetable?" Dick asked.

"It moves it up by two days. It's a good thing you guys went to the range last night instead of putting it off." Pete said.

"OK< so what's the plan now?" Dick asked.

"You guys are leaving in an hour. Did you get those coordinates I asked for?" Pete inquired.

"Yeah I did, Billy's got them." Dick replied.

"BILLY" Pete called out. He came running into the office. "Get those coordinates over to flight operations immediately. The pilot is going to need them, so they don't drop these guys in the wrong spot."

"I'm on it Boss." Billy answered as he headed back out the door.

"Dick, get your boys ready and have them at the chopper pad in an hour." Pete ordered, "And Dick…. Be careful. If it looks like you're not going to be able to pull this off, call 'no joy' and come home. I would rather take flak from command than have to write letters to your families. I've had to write too many of them lately."

"I understand Pete, we'll do the best we can, you know that. But I'm not going to take any unnecessary chances." Dick replied as he headed for the door.

An hour later the team had assembled at the chopper pad and was waiting on the chopper when a jeep pulled to a halt across the small trail that led to the pad. A man in civilian clothes got out and walked towards them.

"Hi I'm John Murphey, your new C.I.A. contact." He said sticking out his hand.

"It's nice to meet you Mr. Murphey, what can I do for you?" Dick said as he shook Murphey's hand.

"Well Captain, as you have probably figured out I'm taking over for Dobbs. It seems he has a small problem with giving all the details. Like that last mission, he knew that those airmen were going to be there, but he didn't think it was important enough to tell you about it. Those at command thought it best if he be detailed to another area." Murphey said after the introductions.

"OK.... That answers that question. But it doesn't answer my first question, what can I do for you?" Dick replied suspiciously.

"Right now, nothing. I just wanted to introduce myself." Murphey said, "But if you could.... When you get back, could you give me a run down on what happened on this mission I would really appreciate it."

"OK, I think we can arrange for that to happen." Dick said with a lopsided grin. The two men continued to talk until they were interrupted by the arrival of the chopper. They shook hands and parted ways.

Within minutes they were airborne and on their way to whatever the fates had in store. As they flew high above the landscape, Kelly was once again impressed with how these simple farmers were able to figure out how to use the contours of the land to such great value. The rice paddies were laid out much like a jigsaw puzzle with every piece perfectly fitted to the piece next to it. It was a beautiful mosaic set in various shades of green and brown.

Soon the lowlands gave way to the low coastal mountains. These were very lust and green. On flights like this Kelly enjoyed just looking at the countryside and taking in the beauty of land he had never seen the likes of before. From up in the chopper it was hard to believe that there was a war going on down there. Things seemed so calm and peaceful.

The chopper circled a meadow that seemed to be nice and flat but when the chopper went to set down the pilot discovered that it was a field of elephant grass. He hovered the chopper as close to the grass as he dared and indicated for the team to jump. One by one they dropped from the skids of the chopper, only to discover that it was about a fifteen-foot drop to the ground. They all landed with a grunt. Luckily no one broke anything. As soon as the last man jumped the chopper rotated away and the team was on their own.

It took them a few minutes to get organized, but they were soon on their way out of the grass. Each man carried a machete for cutting trails through thick vines and tall grass. They took turns cutting their way towards the edge of the forest, once they got there they were able to move at a quicker pace. It seemed like it took forever to cut their way out of the grass. They then started climbing an old water course. The water course contained huge boulders that, in some places, they had to climb around. When they reached the top of the water course the walking became much easier because there was a trail that crossed it and continued in the direction they wanted to go.

They could tell by the under growth that no one had been on the trail for quite some time. Now they covered the distance at a rapid pace. Since the bulk of the mountains ran in a generally north-south direction staying on the ridgetops was not always the direction that would help them. On several occasions it became necessary to traverse a wide valley. At these times they spread out so as not to make targets of themselves.

Finally, they came to the ridge above the compound. They stayed back in the trees but had a good clear view of the camp. The compound appeared much as they had seen in the pictures that they had been studying. The buildings were more permanent than the ones at Major Tau's compound with tile roofs and wooden sides. The main building did resemble a plantation manner house with white columns in the front and a circular brick drive. They observed several soldiers lounging on the front porch without any form of armament. The teamed assumed that they were off duty and just relaxing. They continued to observe the camp as long as the light would permit. They had been able to count a force of about thirty soldiers at the compound. This coincided with what the rangers had counted. It was decided that they would observe the camp one more day to be sure that all the information they had been given was accurate.

It was further decided that they should move their camp further back into the trees to avoid detection. Without hesitation they moved to the back side of the ridge where their movements couldn't accidently be seen from the compound.

During the next day Kelly scouted the ridge for a nest. He finally found what he was looking for, a small depression that was surrounded by small boulders with an unobstructed view of the entire compound. He could even see the roving patrols and learned what their approximate routes were. That way if they got too close to whoever was going in he could knock them off before they had a chance to sound the alarm.

Finally, the time had come for the team to do what they had been sent to do. In a huddled conference it was decided that Slick would spot for Kelly since he was going to be a father soon and no one wanted to be responsible for leaving his child an orphan. It was further decided that Scuzzy Bill would be the cover man and stay at the edge of the perimeter to give cover fire if it was needed. That left Dick and Mense to go in and get their package. This would only be right since they were the strongest of the group and could carry their package out. Dick checked the syringe one last time before they departed.

"When we get back, you two are buying the beer." Dick said to Kelly and Slick as he departed.

"Isn't that just like him, to stick us with the bill when he has all the fun." Kelly said to slick.

"Yep" was all Slick said as he nodded his head a slight grin teased his lips. Slick and Kelly sat in the camp for about an hour before moving into position. Kelly carefully mounted the scope and locked it in, then he reached for a silencer, only to discover that he had left it in his ruck sack. He whispered to Slick to go back and get for him. Slick immediately started off to get it. A short while later Kelly heard a small racket in the bushes. "Damn Slick, you're about a clumsy fool." Kelly thought. Moments later he felt someone move in close to him.

"Give me the silencer Slick." Kelly said.

"You won't be needing it Kelly." A strange but familiar voice said. Kelly's first instinct was to turn and fight, but then he felt the gun barrel in this back.

"Dobbs?" Kelly said questioningly, "What the hell are you doing here?"

"Protecting my interests." Dobbs replied, "Now real easy like pass me back your rifle, and don't get any ideas because I'm not alone." Kelly begrudging did as he was told.

"Where's Slick? Did you kill him?" Kelly snarled.

"No, we didn't kill him, but he will have a headache when he wakes up." Dobbs replied.

"What about the rest of the team, you going to kill them?" Kelly asked. "Not if we can take them alive. Now stand up and turn around." Dobbs instructed. Kelly stood up and turned around, he felt more than saw several other men in the immediate area. He then felt the rope being tightened to the point that it was cutting off the circulation in his hands.

Someone grabbed him by the arm and started pulling him in the direction of the compound. After about an hour of stumbling along, bumping into trees and a few other abuses they came to the edge of the outer boundary of the compound where they stopped. Before long a sentry challenged them, Dobbs answered him in perfect Vietnamese which totally surprised Kelly. After a few moments of speaking they continued to the main building in the compound. They mounted the steps and Kelly was pushed down into one of the chairs.

"Don't get comfortable, you won't be here that long." Dobbs said looking at Kelly with a grin that said, 'look at me I bested you'.

"You treasonous bastard." Kelly snarled back at him, Dobbs just laughed and walked away. Soon they drug Slick up the steps and just let him flop. There was a large gash just above his right eye that had been bleeding but had now stopped. The only sign of life that Kelly could see was the steady rise and fall of his chest. He kept straining at the ropes that bound his hands but could not feel any give in them.

If he could somehow get some slack in the ropes, then maybe he would have a chance of escaping. It seemed the more he tried to loosen them the tighter they became. He wasn't sure what was worse the humiliation of being caught or the feeling of total helplessness at not knowing what was going to happen to him. That was the scariest feeling Kelly knew.

Then there was Dobbs, he would love to get his hands around that neck of his and choke him until he turned green, never mind blue. The anger he felt at being betrayed by one of his own was almost more than he could stand. How anyone could betray his own country was a concept so foreign to Kelly that he refused himself to think about it.

A short distance away voices in the dark drew Kelly's attention. Within moments he saw Dick and Mense being led in at the end of a rope. Their hands were tied behind their backs just as his were. The only one he hadn't seen was Scuzzy Bill, was it possible that they hadn't found him yet? Or had they killed him? As the other two members of the team came into the light, the saw Kelly and Mense. Kelly looked into Dicks eyes and a silent question passed between them, 'How could this have happened?'. Dick just shook his head in bewilderment. Kelly silently mouthed Dobbs. Dick just looked at him until the door of the building opened and Dobbs stepped out on the porch.

"Dobbs…. What are you doing here?" Dick exclaimed, a look of total disbelief on his face.

"What are you guys doing, reading from the same script? That's the same question that Kelly asked when he first saw me. You guys really do need new material." Dobbs said then started laughing.

"You bastard, I am going to kill you." Dick screamed at him.

"Not so fast there Captain. I'm the only one that's keeping you alive right now. You guys are worth a fortune to me and I intend to collect. You have been a thorn in the side of Hanoi for a long time and now I, Julius P. Dobbs, am going to deliver you to them. Of course, I'll be getting some help from the North Vietnamese Army, they're providing the transportation and guard services." Dobbs said gloating.

Just then the front door opened again, and General van Cho stepped out. He looked at each one and lightly tapped Slick in the ribs. He turned and said something over his shoulder to an aid inside the door who quickly ran down the hall. A few minutes later a second man emerged from the house and started examining Slick.

"Hey leave him alone." Dick yelled.

"Be patient young man, I'm a doctor." The man said. Dick calmed down a bit but was still agitated.

"Where did you learn to speak English?" Dick asked, still concerned about Slick.

"I was raised in California from the time I was two. My parents were allowed to enter the country right after the war." the doctor said as he continued his examination of Slick.

"Where did you get your training?" Dick asked.

"I did my undergrad work at U.C.L.A., my residency at Mount Sinai in L.A. and my doctorate at Boston General." the doctor replied, "I understand your concern…. But please let me do my work."

"Sir is he going to be OK?" Kelly asked.

"Yes, I think so, but to be sure I'll need to take x-rays to ensure that he doesn't have a skull fracture. Who did this to this man?" the doctor asked.

"One of my men got a little overzealous." Dobbs injected. Just then the General spoke to his guard and he pointed out the man who had taken down Slick. The general said something in Vietnamese and the soldier saluted and left.

"Gentlemen…. Please allow me to apologize for this unfortunate occurrence. I also know why you are here and that is to kidnap me in hopes of getting me to divulge information that will be helpful to your cause. Let me assure you that will not happen." The general said smugly, "You are now my prisoners and as such you will be treated humanely, and we will notify the international red cross that we have you, but you will receive no mail. For the benefit of my guards I will get an interpreter until you learn our language. Given the stubbornness of your government I think it would be a good guess that you're going to be here a while." General Van Cho recited, "Oh, and gentlemen I do owe you a thank you since you were the team that eliminated a problem for us."

"General, sir.... what problem would that be?" Kelly asked.

"Why the problem of Major Tau. He had become such a bother. We found out that he was making deals with the outer lying villages and if they didn't agree to support him and his group he would simply kill them. It didn't take long for the word to get around of what he had done, and all the other villages fell in line." The general explained, "Then we found out that he was making alliances with other groups to carve out their own kingdom we knew he had to go and thankfully you took care of it for us."

"General.... If you will excuse me but, how did you learn to speak English so well?" Dick asked.

"I was raised in San Francisco until I until was in college and read one of Uncle Ho's speeches. Then I had to meet him, when I did, I was so enthralled with him that I knew that I had to follow him. So, you see I'm actually from America and I have come to detest the western way of life and as a result I have come to detest you." General said with a note of finality, "Now gentlemen you are going to tell me everything I want to know or suffer the consequences.

"The only thing you'll get from me is my name, rank and serial number." Kelly spat, "You're almost as bad as Dobbs, traitors both." With out any kind of warning the general backhanded Kelly across the mouth.

"Insolence will not be tolerated from you or any of you. Do I make myself clear?" General Van Cho snarled. Kelly looked at him with murder in his eyes and just spit at his feet. This earned Kelly another smack in the mouth.

"You're real brave when you have us trussed up like a pig. Untie me and try it. I'll rip you're head off and crap down your neck.it." Kelly snarled as he tried to get up. The general just kicked him in the stomach, knocking the breath out of him. "You coward." He screamed at the general, then his head exploded in pain because one of the guards hit him in the back of the head with a rifle butt. All Kelly could see was the floor coming up to smack him in the face and there was nothing he could do about it.

"Gentlemen let that be a lesson to you all, insolence will cause you to pay a price." The general said, "Now if you cooperate, you will be treated much better than you are being treated now. If you don't cooperate, the consequences will be rough on you. Now then, Captain Van Meter, since you have witnessed what the consequences of non-cooperation are can I count on you for answers?"

Dick looked at the general with such hatred that it sent a shiver up Dobbs back. As he had watched the scenario play out on the porch, he was sure that Kelly would be the hardheaded one that would cause the most trouble. He had informed General Van Cho that if he could break Kelly that the others would probably follow. But, when the soldier cracked Kelly in the back of the head with the rifle butt it even made his head hurt. Dobbs knew that Kelly was tough, but he was surprised when he was able to drag himself back up to a sitting position after the blow to the head.

"Captain Van Meter…. I'm waiting for your answer." The general said with a slight bit of frustration in his voice.

Dick looked at the bloodied Kelly sat up to his full height and said, "Richard Earl Ven Meter, Captain, U.S. Army, O1375824." This earned Dick the back of the general's hand. Blood trickled down his chin, but he sat straight and ridged.

The general now turned his attention to Mense. "Young man are you going to be the smart one of the bunch? Are you the one that tells me what I want to know?" Mense looked at him and started laughing. The general was obviously confused. "What do you find so funny?"

"You.... you think so little of us. You think that a few slaps and a little blood will scare us enough to betray our country. You're an idiot." Mense spat back.

"You insolent little brat. I ought to just kill you all right now." The general screamed at him.

"Yeah, you do that.... Then where will you get your information? From Dobbs.... He doesn't know squat and dead men can't tell you anything." Mense replied. This infuriated the general to a point that all he could do was scream and punch Mense with a closed fist. The more he hit Mense the more Mense laughed.

Finally, Mense keeled over unconscious from the beating. The general said something to one of the soldiers and he saluted and left. A few minutes later, several soldiers came up on the porch and very roughly picked up Mense and started dragging him away. The other soldiers jerked Kelly and Dick to their feet and started marching them off in the same direction as Mense had been drug.

They were marched over to a different building that didn't seem to have very many lights in it. The strange thing about the building was that it was brick and concrete. The soldiers stopped them just outside the door and then took then in one at a time. When Kelly's turn came to go through the entry door he was surprised to see that it was a jail with iron bars and no windows in the cells. There were no cots in the cells just a concrete floor.

The guards indicated that they were to turn and face the wall. A few minutes later Dobbs entered and asked where Scuzzy Bill was. Kelly and Dick exchanged glances but didn't say anything, they just quietly chuckled to themselves.

"There's still hope" Kelly thought to himself, "If they don't know where Bill is then maybe he can get us out of here."

# CHAPTER 15

*A single event can awaken within us
A stranger totally unknown to us*

*Antoine de Saint-Exupary
(1900-!944)*

The stay in Laos was brief, just a few weeks. But in those few weeks Kelly took more beatings than he ever thought he would be able to endure. It seemed like he was being beaten just for breathing. They would always ask the same questions and he would give the same answers, his name, rank, and serial number. Then he would be punched or kicked or some other form of abuse until he passed out. This seemed to be a daily ritual, but one day it changed. Instead of going to the interrogation room they led him outside into the courtyard, Mense, Dick Van Meter, and Slick were already there. They looked at each other with the same question in their eyes, what's going on now?

"No talking!" the soldier in command screamed at them. They stood in a rough line waiting for whatever was coming. What was first and foremost in their minds was the question of whether this was going to be their last moments on this earth. They thought about the good and the bad they had done in their lives. Was there really a God? If there was would he merciful to them? Had they done enough good to outweigh the bad?

Then General Van Cho strolled into the courtyard, he was dressed not in his military uniform but instead in civilian clothes. He looked at each one from behind aviator sunglasses, not saying anything. The team, or what was left of it, were still in the same clothes they had been captured in. Their boots had been taken by the guards and their shirts were ripped and torn from the abuse of the questioning. There was dried blood matted in their hair and on their clothes.

"Gentlemen, you have had a small bit of a rough time. But my interrogators say they can't stand to be in the same room with you anymore because you stink. So, as a gesture of good will I am going to allow you to bathe and clean up a little bit." The general said in a calm voice.

He then signaled to a soldier at the corner, a moment later several soldiers came around the corner with a firehose. They attached it to a hydrant and began shooting water at the team. After a few moments they stopped, and the team was ordered to turn around, then again, they were sprayed with the firehose. The stream was so powerful that it almost knocked them down. They stood as best they could, but the stream of water caused them to lose their footing and they fell. The guards that were looking on began to laugh at the sight. Soon the water stopped.

Now the team was not only wet, but now they were covered in the mud from the courtyard. They were a very poor looking group. They were then ordered to follow a soldier and to do as they were told. They were marched to a far back building where they saw multiple bamboo cages like they had seen the airmen put into. But these were different, they had long poles attached to them. They were ordered to pick them up and follow the guards. The guards led them to the main courtyard where several vehicles were parked. General Van Cho and Dobbs were waiting for them.

"You stay here is done. You are being transferred to a P.O.W. camp." The general said.

"And I will get my reward." Dobbs injected then laughed.

"Dobbs... if I ever see you again I'm going to kill you." Kelly snarled. This was greeted by a rifle butt to the back of the head, which caused Dobbs to start laughing again.

"You shouldn't threaten an honored guest Mister Broadwick." Dobbs said smugly, "It is most impolite."

"Dobbs.... I wasn't threatening you, I was making you a promise." Kelly said through gritted teeth.

"Enough of this, pick up those cages and follow the trucks. If you're thinking of escape, I would forget it. There will be guards surrounding you and if you try to escape you will be shot. Is that understood?" the general said in a commanding voice.

The team looked at each other and picked up the cages. Then began walking towards the trucks. As they approached the truck several soldiers climbed out and formed up on each side of them. The truck started moving forward and they were forced to follow. They kept walking for hours before the truck stopped. The interpreter told them to put the cages down and sit down in the middle of the road. They were admonished not to talk unless spoken to directly. They just looked at the interpreter and nodded.

This became the norm for the team, walk hours carrying the cages. When met a convoy of trucks they would go to the side of the road and sit down. The soldiers in the passing convoy would spit at them and sometimes do other disgusting things. The team was humiliated in unimaginable ways. They were forced to sleep sitting up in the cages because there wasn't enough room for them to lie down. When they would meet villagers along the road they had stones thrown at them and they were cursed at by little old ladies. The only saving grace was that they didn't understand what the villagers were saying.

Finally, after what seemed like months of walking they were met by a convoy from the prison. After a short but heated exchange between the commander of the prison detail and the commander of the original detail the team was put on a truck and taken to the prison. None of the team knew what to expect. They knew how the Americans treated prisoners, but if how they had been treated was any example of how they were going to be treated this was going to be a long wait for rescue.

When they reached the prison, they were instructed to undress and were given striped pants and shirts. Once again, they were subjected to the firehose shower and assigned to individual cells. The cells were stark and damp with no toilet facilities they were given a bucket to take care of their business. Their n mattress was a long cloth bag that had been filled with rice husks. They were given a wool blanket with the admonishment that if it was ever discovered to have any part missing they would lose the privilege of having a blanket.

After they had been there a month they were taken to a room and introduced to an International Red Cross worker. It was the first time the team had been together since they arrived. It was a joyous reunion. There was a lot of hugs. When they finally settled down, they answered the questions the aid worker asked. They then told the aid worker about the guards stealing all their personal effects. They took the teams wallets, their watches, wedding rings, anything of value. They also told the aid worker about having to walk without shoes of any kind.

The aid worker, Mister Sven Sorensen, was Swedish and a national of a neutral nation. He had heard of this happening many times before. He had filed out complaint after complaint and watched them be wadded up and thrown away. He had complained to his superiors and they said it was just the price of war. This made him angry because no one was trying to do anything to stop the thievery. But he would submit the complaint and hope for the best. He also asked about the scars and the cuts that were still healing. Dick and Kelly told him about the rough treatment at the hands of General Van Cho. They also told him about the cages and the poor food they were receiving. Mense didn't say much since he was nursing a broken jaw also the result of General Van Cho's rough treatment. This revelation outraged Sorensen, he asked the guard to have the prison commander meet with him immediately. The prison commander, General Nguyen, was a seemingly pleasant man who was getting close to retirement age. He was given the prison job because there was little to do except some paperwork. He had served in the North Vietnamese Army since he was a young man and had worked himself up through the ranks. All he wanted to do was finish his time, retire, and live a happy life. But these American pilots and soldiers were proving to be quite the handful.

"Mister Sorensen, what seems to be the trouble" the general asked. "General Nguyen, this man has a broken jaw and has not received proper medical attention. That is a serious violation of the Geneva Convention. I must insist that he be seen immediately, or I will have to bring it to the attention of the World, that North Viet Nam is abusing prisoners of war." Sorensen stated.

"Yes, Mister Sorensen I quite agree with you, this is not acceptable. I will have him treated right now." The general said. He turned to one of the guards, said something in Vietnamese and the guard rushed out. "Van Cho is going to have to be more careful." He thought.

A short time later a man of about Dick's age came through the door carrying a medical bag. He began to examine Mense's jaw. To say that he was surprised at the swelling and discoloration after so long a time was an understatement.

"I'm Doctor Ky. When did this happen?" he asked, still examining the jaw. "About a month and a half ago. He was beaten unconscious by General Van Cho over at Tam Lo Loc. Where did you learn English? You speak it very well with hardly any accent at all." Dick said.

"I lived in Hawaii for about fifteen years when I was young then my family moved to California." The doctor replied. He turned and said something in Vietnamese to the general then turned back to Dick. "Your friend has a very serious problem. To fix it is going to require surgery. I can't guarantee that he'll be as good as he was before he broke it, but he will have a lot less problem eating."

"Anything would be an improvement doctor. And while you're at it see if you can make him better looking. He's about as ugly as they come." Dick said with a chuckle. Mense gave him the middle finger salute, the rest of the team chuckled.

The doctor ushered Mense away and the team was again alone with Mister Sorensen, except for the guards. "Mister Sorensen, there was a fifth member of our team. We haven't heard anything about him, as far as we know he didn't get captured when we did, is there any way you can find out about him?" Dick asked.

"I can try, what was his name." Sorensen replied.

"William Butler Johnson. He was our cover man and when we got captured I think he may have gotten away." Dick said.

"OK, I'll check with your unit and find out what I can. I'll let you know when I come back next month." Sorensen promised. The whole team thanked him as they were being ushered back to their cells.

Days went by and no one heard anything about Mense. One day the doctor came around and stopped to check on each man in his cell. When he got to Dick's cell he passed on by, he did the same to Kelly's cell. When he came to Slick's cell he told the guard to open the door. A few moments after he entered there was a lot of commotion and guards running down the cell block. A few moments later Dick and Kelly saw them carrying Slick on a stretcher. He had a very bloody face and head. Neither one of them could see much through the observation door at the top of the cell door.

"Kelly, did you see that?" Dick called through the small opening.

"Yeah.... What'd they do to him? I didn't hear anything, did you?" Kelly called back.

"No, I didn't hear a sound." Dick replied.

Just then the small door slammed shut in Dick's face. Now they were left to wonder and worry about another member of their team. Were the North Vietnamese killing them off one by one? Who would be next? Had his training prepared him for something like this? Being Isolated for twenty-three out of twenty-four hours was hard on a man's mind. He has nothing to do but think and sometimes his mind can play tricks on him. Was Kelly feeling the same things he was? As far as he could tell Kelly had a very strong mind and could resist psychological torture.

"Kelly.... Don't let them break you." Dick screamed. He didn't know if Kelly heard him or not but at least he tried to help him.

"They won't." came the faint response. This made Dick feel on top of the world. He wasn't alone, he still had Kelly. But what about Mense and Slick? Are they going to be alright? Were they maybe already dead? How could he tell Slick's wife that he couldn't save him?

The thought of having to tell Slick's wife that he had failed one of his best friends sent Dick into tears. He cried deep racking sobs. But no matter how much he cried it wasn't going to change the fact that Slick was dead. How could he bear the shame of allowing his whole team to get captured? But in reality, it wasn't his fault, that damn Dobbs betrayed them. Them and the entire United States of America. Right then and there he swore that he would live beyond this and then he would find Dobbs and kill him…. Slowly.

"Kelly…. I'm going to kill Dobbs." Dick screamed.

"No, you're not…. At least not without me." Kelly called back. Suddenly Dick heard the key in the lock of his door. What was going to happen to him now? He crawled as far back away from the door as he could. The door opened and the light from behind the figure wouldn't allow him to see who it was. The figure was too large to be one of his Vietnamese captors.

"Stand up…. You're coming with me." It was a voice Dick didn't recognize. He slowly and apprehensively stood up, not knowing what to expect. The figure turned and stepped out into the corridor. Slowly Dick followed him until he got just outside the door and he was struck in the side of the head. He fell to his knees and became immediately nauseated. Then he saw the blood dripping onto the floor.

"That's what you get for trying to escape." the voice said.

"I wasn't trying to escape…. You told me to follow you!" Dick yelled at him. This outburst was greeted by the butt end of a rifle. Dick could feel the loose teeth and tasted the metallic taste of blood. He spit blood on the floor and received a kick in the ribs, this was almost more than he could take. His anger at the abuse that was being heaped on him only served to strengthen his resolve not to be broken. "These bastards won't break me." He thought. As he tried to return to a sitting position he was again kicked in the ribs and was certain that something had just been broken. The pain was excruciating, but he refused to give them the satisfaction of knowing that they had hurt him.

"We are your lords and masters, you do only what we tell you to do and speak only when we tell you to speak. You will say only things that will please us, or you will suffer more of the same kind of treatment that you are now receiving. Do you understand?" the voice said. Dick only nodded because he was gritting his teeth against the pain. "Very good.... You learn quickly. I am Colonel Nguyen Ky of the People's Army of Viet Nam. When you feel better we'll sit down and have a little chat. Put him back in his cell."

Two guards roughly grabbed Dick and drug him back into his cell and then let him flop onto the hard floor. This sent a new wave of nausea through Dick. He vowed that if he ever got out of this alive that he would see these bastards hung. The door slammed shut, but he could hear their muffled voices through the door. Then he heard a loud scream like someone being hurt.

"Kelly", he thought, "They're going after Kelly." Then he heard Kelly's voice as he cussed at the colonel. "Give them hell Kelly." Dick thought, and he smiled. The yelling and commotion in the passageway continued for a short while longer. Then he heard the slam of the steel door and he assumed it was the door to Kelly's cell.

After what seemed like just a few minutes Dick heard a faint voice calling him. Even though if hurt terribly he sat up and looked around. He couldn't see any place the voice could be coming from. Then he strained to hear the voice again because he thought he recognized it. It was Kelly!

"Yes, I hear you. Are you alright?" Dick called back.

"Don't yell they'll hear you. Get close to the wall and we can hear better." Kelly replied. Dick painfully scooted over close to the wall and leaned his head against it.

"I'm close, can you hear me now?" dick said in a conversational tone. "Yeah, almost as good as when you were yelling. We need to find a way out of here, I'm not going to die in this sewer." Kelly said.

"I know, I don't want that either. Kelly, I'm so sorry to get you into this. I should have turned this mission down, but my ego got in the way. I'm so sorry." Dick said as tears ran down his face.

"Don't worry about that now, I'll kick your ass after we get out of here. Right now, we need to get as much information as we can about this place, so we can plan. Do you know Morse code?" Kelly asked.

"Yeah, why?" Dick asked, not knowing what Kelly had in mind.

"Do you have a pipe running through the back wall of your cell?" Kelly asked.

"Yeah, but it runs tight against the wall." Dick replied.

"Try tapping out a message on it and see if you can get a response." Kelly suggested.

"OK' Dick replied. Dick hauled himself to a standing position and moved towards the back of his cell. In Morse code he tapped out, 'can anyone hear me'. He waited a few moments then tapped it out again. Again, he waited a few moments and re-tapped the message. To his elation he got the response of, 'yes I can'. Dick could hardly contain himself. He quickly started tapping questions like who are you and where are you. These replies sent his emotions soaring, now he knew that he could communicate with other people and that he and Kelly were not alone. He found out that there were six other captives and they were all navy flyers. Five of them were being held in same cell block as Kelly and himself, but another one, John McCain, was being held in the infirmary because of injuries he got when his plane went down.

Dick gently moved back over to the wall and asked Kelly if he got any of the conversation. Kelly said that yes, he did, he got the whole thing. Now Dick's pain and despair wasn't so bad. His sprits had been lifted at the knowledge that they weren't alone. Now there was a chance.

Within hours they had set up a network of communication where each prisoner could communicate with someone else. The guards heard the tapping on the pipe but didn't pay any attention to it. Through the weeks and months that were to come this would prove to be a saving grace for all of them. When the months turned into years they used their network to buoy up each other when they started feeling low and hopeless.

Sometimes they would use the network to celebrate significant milestones in their lives like anniversaries or their children's birthday, or even their own birthdays. The network became a lifeline for the captives. Then one afternoon, they were brought from their cells to a large room where a large contingent of reporters and cameras were waiting.

"Gentlemen, this is the last day you will spend as guests of the government of Viet Nam. Your government has given in to our demands and you are being released back to them." Colonel Ky told them. This was met with skepticism. "You will be allowed to shower, and you will be given clean clothes to wear for your flight home. Mister Sorensen, of the International Red Cross will be your liaison for these last few hours. If you wish anything give him your requests and we will do what we can to make them a reality."

When Mister Sorensen walked into the room with no guards around him the men knew that this was for real and they burst out in shouts of joy. They hugged one another and in some cases were so overwhelmed by the news that all they could do was cry. They were tears of joy, finally they were going home. The thought of it was tempered by the thought of what had happened while they were gone. Children had grown, spouses had aged, and they had become emotionally harder.

They had learned not to take anything at face value, their captors had used many psychological weapons against them in an attempt to get them to do what they wanted. But they had remained true to what they believed in. While in captivity, they had suffered beatings, been deprived of food, and tortured. But, through it all they had remained steadfastly true to their country.

Kelly and Dick were standing a bit apart from the pilots when the door opened again and Slick and Mense walked in. They looked very gaunt and disheveled, but when they saw Dick and Kelly they ran towards them. The four hugged and cried on each other's shoulders. Somehow the message got through, THEY WERE GOING HOME!

# CHAPTER 16

*Suffering has always been with us,*
*Does it really matter in what form it comes?*
*All that matters is how we bear it*
*and how We fit it into our lives.*

*Etty Hillesum*
*(1914-1943)*

The next few hours were spent being cleaned and groomed for return to civilized society. They were all given showers, haircuts and clean uniforms provided by their respective services. Then they were whisked off to the airport under the cover of night so as not to arouse public demonstrations against them.

The next stop for the team was Yokohama Air Force Base in Japan. The other captives were sent to Clark Field in the Philippines. Here they were debriefed about what had happened to them during their captivity. They were given the chance to name names and describe in detail some of the atrocities that were heaped on them while in captivity.

When Kelly's turn came he started out by telling his questioner, Captain James McDonald about Dobbs. Captain McDonald told him not to worry about Dobbs because he had already been dealt with. This confused Kelly, he asked how.

"Kelly, Dobbs is dead. He was killed in Thailand shortly after you were captured." Captain McDonald stated.

"Who killed him, us or them?" Kelly asked.

"I killed him." Said a voice from behind him. Kelly snapped around to see Scuzzy Bill standing just inside the door with a big grin on his face.

"BILL!" Kelly screamed and jumped up. They met in the middle of the room and embraced as two long lost brothers. There had been many a night Kelly had wondered what had happened to him.

"Have you seen Dick or Mense or Slick yet?" Kelly asked.

"No, but I'm hoping his reaction will be as welcoming as yours was." Bill replied. Bill had tears in his eyes as he remembered the night of the capture. "Can you ever forgive me for not covering you guys like I should have done?"

"Bill there is nothing to forgive. Your job was to cover us if there was any shooting, but there wasn't any so how could you know? You did exactly what you were supposed to do, you stayed alive and didn't get captured. How long after we got caught were you able to get out of there?" Kelly asked.

"After I saw them march you guys in, I laid low and snuck back into the jungle. It took me about three days to get back to the Green Beret camp. From there I choppered back to Duc Pho. I told Pete and division G-2 what I'd seen and at first G-2 didn't believe me. Pete contacted Murphey to see if he could track down Dobbs, but he was unsuccessful. That was the only time I've ever seen Pete react to bad news, he actually sat down and cried over you guys. The next day I told Pete I was going back after you guys, but he wouldn't let me. He insisted that he was going along. He played spotter and I took the shot. Then no more Dobbs, no more problems." Bill explained.

"Thank you, I just knew there was something wrong about him. I just couldn't put my finger on it. He was working both sides of the fence trying to get rich at our expense, the bastard." Kelly snarled.

"Look, you've got work to do here Captain…" Bill started. "Wrong…. I'm only a lieutenant." Kelly corrected.

"NO…. you're wrong. Pete put you in for the promotion about a month after your capture. He also put Dick, Mense, and Slick in for promotion. Even I got one.' Bill said pointing to lieutenant's bar on his collar.

"Well I'll be damned." Kelly laughed, "You mean to tell me that I'm now a captain?"

"Yep…. Dick's a major and Slick and Mense are First Lieutenants." Bill said as he pushed out his chest.

"Don't be getting all full of yourself, Bill. I still out rank you." Kelly said, then they both started laughing.

"What about Pete, where's he now?" Kelly asked.

"Well after his tour was up he came back to the states and retired. The last I heard he was working for some chemical company down in Texas." Bill replied.

"Gentlemen, I hate to break up this reunion, but I do have a few more questions for Captain Broadwick." Captain McDonald injected.

"Sure, I'm sorry Captain, I was just so anxious to see my friends again." Bill said apologetically.

"That's OK lieutenant believe it or not I do understand." Captain McDonald replied with a smile, "I'll make sure that the five of you have a special table at the officer's club tonight. How's that?"

"Great, I'll see you after while Kelly." Bill said as he left.

"OK Kelly is there any questions you have for me?" the captain asked. "Yeah, can I call my family now?" Kelly asked. The captain got a stricken look on his face.

"Kelly, I'm sorry, but that won't be possible." He said quietly, knowing the storm that was about to come.

"WHY NOT?" Kelly shouted, angry that he was being kept incognito from the whole world.

"Well it's not that we don't want you to talk to them, it's that it's just not possible." He said. This didn't pacify Kelly at all.

"No, I can't accept that I can't talk to them. I want to know the reason right now." Kelly said loudly as he stood leaning on his fists on the table.

"Alright…. If you must know, they're dead. They were killed in a car crash about two years ago." The captain said quietly.

Kelly just looked at him in disbelief. How could that be, his parents were fine when he left. How could they be dead? Kelly slowly sank back down into his chair. His mind was going a hundred miles a second trying to take it all in. Then he felt the tears welling up in his eyes and he began to sob. They were deep soul racking sobs that were the expression of his breaking heart. The people that he had loved all his life were now gone and he had no one.

But wait he did have someone, he had Doris. She promised to wait for him. He knew that all through his captivity she had been on his mind and he knew that she would be there when he finally came home. All was not lost, he did have something to start over with.

The captain let him have some time to digest the bad news about his parents. His heart went out to him, after spending a little over four years as a prisoner of war then to find out that his family was gone had to be quite a blow. Never had he felt so inadequate, he wished he had a magic touch that would make all the pain go away. But, since he couldn't do that he would do whatever he could to try to ease the pain.

"Kelly is there anyone else you would like to call?" he asked quietly. Kelly slowly raised his head from his hands and looked at him.

"Yes, Captain McDonald, there is. Can you get a call through to my girlfriend, Doris Livingstone in Plano, Texas?" Kelly replied.

"I don't see why not. I'll go and see what I can do." Captain McDonald replied, "Since we're the same rank, please call me Jim."

After Jim had left, Kelly was still reeling from the news of his parent's death. What was he going to do now? There was so much to consider like what kind of shape the ranch was in after two years; had anyone been caring for the place? Who was paying the bills? Where did the money for the bills come from? Could he stay in the army? Should he stay in the army? Did he know enough to take over the ranch? These were all questions running through his mind when Jim came back into the room.

"Kelly, it seems like I can only bring you bad news. Doris has married someone else. I spoke with her mother and she said that Doris waited two years before she got married to someone she had met at work. She's been married for a little over three years." Jim informed him. He watched as Kelly's shoulders just slumped down. It seemed as if he was now a broken man, Jim felt sorry for him and wished more than anything that he could give him some good news, but it seemed that all he was bringing was bad news.

"Jim…. Do you think we could try to reach my uncle in Mesquite, Texas?" Kelly asked quietly.

"Yeah…. Sure…. What's his name?" Jim asked.

"George Broadwick on Morrison Road in Mesquite, Texas." Kelly replied hopefully. Jim left and said he would do everything he could to get the call through. Kelly remembered his uncle George well, he had been told stories of how he had served with General Patton during World War II. He had a clear picture in his mind of his Uncle George.

George Broadwick had served with Patton's Third Armor in France as a tank commander. He had two tanks blown out from under him but had refused to leave the battles. When the war was over, he had advanced from a sergeant up to a captain and company commander. He had also been awarded two purple hearts, a bronze star, and a silver star. The men that served under him had nicknamed him 'Galloping George Broadwick', because of the way he always be in a hurry to get somewhere.

The door opened, and Jim signaled for Kelly to follow him. They walked down the hall to another room where several phones had been set up. Jim indicated for Kelly to pick up one of the phones.

"Hello?" Kelly said.

"Is that really you Kelly. Thank God you're out and safe" came the voice of his Uncle George.

"UNCLE GEORGE! GOD AM I GLAD TO HEAR YOUR VOICE." Kelly screamed into the phone. He quickly regained his composure, just hearing his uncle's voice had done wonders for his mood. Now he didn't feel quite as alone. As they chatted Kelly was able to get quite a few of his questions answered about the ranch.

He also found out that he was now a very wealthy man because before he had died his father had signed a contract with an oil company to allow them to drill on the property. Kelly also learned that his uncle had been caring for the ranch in anticipation of Kelly coming home. The conversation lasted for about thirty minutes and at the end after he hung up, Kelly began to cry. It was a release all the emotions he had to keep pent up throughout his captivity, the anger, despair, hopelessness and fear. Jim let him have his private time to cry and get all his tears out of the way so that he could start to heal.

Jim had been warned when he was given the assignment that he would see emotion unlike any he had ever seen. The men he would be dealing with had just spent a long time locked up with no form of communication with the outside world. In their lives some of the people they depended on before their captivity were now dead and it would be a shock to them. Some of their wives will have divorced them, thinking that they were dead and some of their girlfriends will have moved on to other partners. He was told to be prepared for everything from outright violence to quiet acceptance of the situation. Jim had also been told to be prepared for a lot of tears from these men because they have no other way to release what's inside them.

After Kelly had gotten some of his tears out of the way Jim quietly asked if he could continue with their debriefing. Kelly just nodded. Having a degree in psychology, Jim could tell that there was something smoldering just below the surface of Kelly's calm demeanor. Just exactly what it was Jim couldn't guess, but he was hoping to find out so that he could get Kelly the help he didn't know he needed.

When Jim asked about the conditions in the prison he noticed that Kelly began to shake ever so slightly. When he asked about the scar on the side of Kelly's head Kelly shrank down in his chair and refused to answer. To Jim this was a prime indicator that Kelly was suffering from what was called 'battle fatigue' in World War II. In modern day 1975 they called it post-traumatic stress disorder or P.T.S.D. There was no known cure for it except time and that was a very open-ended frame. From what he had read about it, there could be bouts of depression, extremely real dreams that terrified the subject, there could be heavy drug and alcohol use. He decided he would observe the team later over at the officer's club to see how they react to being around large groups.

"Jim, what's going to happen now? My enlistment is up, and I don't know what to do. Should I try to stay in the army or should I go home and take care of my ranch?" Kelly said in way of his asking for advice.

"Well it seems to me that you have a big choice to make. Do you know anyone that you really trust their opinion that you can ask that same question to?" Jim asked.

"Well actually there is, Pete Philmore, he was my company commander in Viet Nam." Kelly replied after some thought.

"I Don't suppose you know where he is now?" Jim asked.

"Well, Scuzzy Bill told me he was working for a chemical company in east Texas. He didn't say the name of it but there can't be that many chemical companies in east Texas." Kelly replied with a hopeful tone.

"A guy named Scuzzy Bill told you this? What kind of name is that?" Jim asked laughing.

"Well, when I joined the outfit, I was told that Bill had a problem with staying close to clean in the field. But as time went on he became better at it, but the name stuck with him." Kelly explained.

"That makes sense I guess." Jim said chuckling, "Did he tell you what chemical company he was working for?"

"No, he didn't, but there can't be that many. Over in East Texas, where I'm from, there is one by the name of Clever Chemical. You might start there, if he doesn't work there they might know where he is. I've been told that most of those people know each other." Kelly said.

"OK, I'll make some calls and see if I can track him down. In the meantime, you and your friends spend some well-deserved time relaxing." Jim told him.

"That sounds like a good plan. Do you know how long we'll be here? I'd really like to go home and visit my parent's graves." Kelly said with tears in his eyes.

"Right now, I can't give you a definite time frame, but I can promise you that it won't be any longer than is necessary." Jim replied as he got up to leave.

"Where do I go now? They've kept me in these hospital clothes since I've gotten here. Is there a P.X. here where I can buy some clothes? Also, where can I get some money, I don't have any." Kelly asked acting a bit confused.

"Well, I tell you what I'm going to do. Would you mind waiting here for a few minutes while I make some calls and then I'll be able to answer all of your questions." Jim said cheerfully. Kelly just said OK and sat back down at the table.

As Jim was walking down the hall, he began to think about what the men he had interviewed had been through. The constant stress, the beatings for no reason, the poor diet and all the rest. He was quite surprised that, psychologically, they were in as good a shape as they were. But he was worried about Kelly. Kelly seemed to be the most detached of all. He seemed to have buried his anger and pain very deeply.

From what he had read about P.T.S.D., Kelly could explode at any time. The only sign he had not shown was the nightmares. But then, since they had only been out of captivity a short time the real trauma of what had happened to him may not have come to the surface yet. But when it does he hoped Kelly would be smart enough to seek help from a doctor and not from drugs or alcohol.

When Jim got back to his office there was a message for him to call Major Stan Adams, the Chief of the Mental Health Service. He picked up the phone and dialed the number.

"Major Adams." A voice said.

"Major Adams, this is Captain McDonald, I just got your message to call. What can I do for you?" Jim said.

"I was just wondering how the de-briefing was going. Can you give me any details on these men?" Major Adams asked.

"To tell you the truth, they all display signs of post-traumatic stress disorder. But, given what they have been through, I would have been more surprised if they didn't show any signs. I am concerned about one of the though, Captain Kelly Broadwick. He seems to be too much in control of what he shows. I think he may be a ticking time bomb. I was about to call and get them all some money and arrange for them to have a table at the officer's club tonight so that they can use each other to lean on. I'm going to arrange for a couple of the attendings to be on hand to observe without them knowing. That way we can get a better sense of what's going on with them." Jim explained.

"That's a good plan, however we don't know how they'll react around a large group of people. If something goes wrong, someone may get hurt. They all know you and may trust you, why don't you go along with them and kind of chaperone them. That way you can fend off anyone that might start any trouble. As a back up I'll be hovering in the background ready to step in if needed." Stan said.

"Stan, that's a good idea. Maybe after they have had a few drinks they'll loosen up and talk more about what they're feeling. Do I need special permission to do this?" Jim asked.

"No, but I'll give it to you if anything goes sideways." Stan chuckled. "Thanks boss." Jim said joining in the chuckle and hanging up the phone.

He then spent the next twenty minutes making arrangements for the team to receive two months pay and clothing vouchers at the P.X. He then called the officer's club and made arrangements for the team to have a table for dinner and drinks afterward. Then he went to give the news to Kelly.

On his way out, he gave his secretary Pete Philmore's name and asked her to track him down. To his surprise his secretary already knew where to find Pete. She said there had been an article in a magazine about him taking over as Chief Operating Officer at Clever Chemical. She also told him that she wouldn't have to track him down because he was already in Tokyo. This news excited Jim more than he could express, now he could get some insight into what these men were like before they were captured. He told her to find him and get him to the officer's club tonight. Just then the door opened and an older man with salt and pepper hair stepped in. He was dressed in a well-tailored gray business suite and had an all-business demeanor about him.

"I understand you have some of my men here." He said.
"I don't know we might, who are you?" Jim asked.
"I'm Colonel Peter Philmore, retired. Formerly with the Special Operations Group of the Americal Division." The man replied with a definite tone of pride.
"Well Colonel Philmore, it's a pleasure to meet you. Sir, I'm Captain James McDonald, I've been interviewing your men since they got here yesterday. I need to talk to you before I can let you see your men. Shall we go into my office." Jim said.

They went into Jim's office and he explained about the diagnoses he had come up with. Pete listened intently and only asked a few questions. By the time they walked back into the reception area Pete had a full understanding of what the team was facing. He also said that whatever his men needed that he would stand good for the bill. He further agreed to meet them at the officer's club at seven o'clock to have dinner and a few drinks. For some reason Jim didn't think it would be just a few drinks.

Pete Left the doctor's office and was quite sure that he too had some degree of P.T.S.D., though not to the extent that his men had it. He remembered hearing about Jackson, the man Kelly replaced, committing suicide. At the time he couldn't understand what had driven him to such a point that he felt that killing himself was his only way out. Now he had a better understanding of the toll combat takes on the mental health of men put in such high stress positions.

Pete thought about Kelly, he seemed to be the one most at risk for such terminal thinking. He made up his mind that he was going to do everything in his power to save Kelly from such a fate. He was now in a position to offer Kelly a way out, an open door. But Pete had to ask himself, would Kelly recognize the offer as a hand up to a better place or would he view it as an offering of guilt on Pete's part. He hoped with all his heart that Kelly would accept his offer and come to work at Cleaver Chemical. That way Pete would be close at hand to render any aid Kelly needed.

Pete looked at his watch and decided it was time to make some phone calls. He first wanted to talk to several of the members of the board at Cleaver Chemical and advise them of what he was doing and how the negotiations in Tokyo were going. He then had to contact his office and get caught up on the latest activities of the various projects he was involved with. With all of this to do he wondered how he could fit it all into his day, but then again, he had forgotten about the time difference, seventeen hours. Then he thought, they had gotten along before he came to the company and they'll get along after he's gone. Right now, he was needed by some men he had become as close to him as if they were his brothers and, in some respects, they were closer.

Pete knew that his evaluation of the men could go a long way in helping to put together a course of action that would benefit all of them. But Pete was most concerned about

Kelly, he had a rough start with his tour, but he had shown no signs of fear, only an innate sense of duty. This bothered Pete because he knew that at some point in time Kelly would break and God only knows what the consequences of that could be. Kelly was a well-trained marksman, but he doubted if Kelly would use his training to do harm to innocent people. On the other hand, there had been Dobbs, he turned out to be a sniveling little traitor who trafficked in information that got people killed. Kelly may have trouble trusting anyone in authority because of it.

This brought up the question of how Kelly would look at him, since he was the commander that sent him on the mission that got him captured. Would Kelly accept that it was a decision that he had made without all the facts or would he look at it as a decision where he was treated as a pawn in a game, an expendable commodity. Either way Pete would find out in about an hour when he met with the team at the officer's club.

Pete was looking forward to seeing the team together once again. Of course, Bumper wouldn't be there, thank God, because he had left before the mission had even been thought of. He thought of Bumper and remembered how the big hulking mass of a man had at times seemed like a small boy enthralled with the mysteries of life. He also remembered Mense, the tough kid from Chicago, he seemed destined to be a brilliant teacher before he got drafted. Now his career as a teacher was in doubt. Pete made a promise to himself that he would do everything he could to make these men's lives the way they had planned.

Finally, it was time to head over to the officer's club and meet the team. Captain McDonald had suggested that the team not know that he was coming, let it be a surprise for them. Captain McDonald had stated that as far as he had been able to determine none of the men thought that Pete had been the cause for their capture. But to be on the safe side there were going to be several other doctors there but not as a part of their group.

The team assembled in Captain McDonald's office and headed over to the club as a group. Since it was just a short walk from the hospital to the club and the night air was warm, it was an enjoyable trek. When they walked in they were greeted by a civilian hostess of Japanese descent. She said that their table was ready with a bit of a Japanese accent and for them to please follow her. As they stepped into the dining room someone called," ATTENTION". Then amid the scraping of chairs and the clink of silverware being set down everyone in the room stood at attention and saluted. They then broke out in applause. The hostess turned and smiled as she too applauded the team. This caught the team completely off guard and they didn't know what to do, they looked back at Jim Mc Donald who was smiling and applauding. Since Dick had been team leader it fell to him to thank the crowd for their applause. He raised his hands for quiet and then he began to speak.

"Fellow officers and guests, I would like to thank you on behalf of myself and my team. This outpouring of appreciation is a bit overwhelming and has caught us completely by surprise. We don't know how to show our appreciation other than to salute you." Dick said. Almost instantly the team snapped to attention and saluted the room. This gesture again drew applause. From the back of the room someone shouted, "hip, hip, hooray" three times and was joined by the gathered crowd, this was followed by more applause. "Thank you again ladies and gentlemen, but we would really like to get a good meal because hospital food stinks." Dick said chuckling. His comment was greeted by mild laughter and several catcalls that agreed with him. The hostess then showed them to a table at the back of the room.

After they were seated, a cocktail waitress came to the table to take their orders. As she was writing down the last order a voice from behind her said, "Add a scotch on the rocks to that." The entire table turned to see Pete standing a short distance away. In short order, the entire team jumped up and rushed him. Before he knew what was going on his hand was being pumped and he was being ushered unceremoniously to the table and placed in a seat someone had dragged over from another table. Everyone was talking at once and Pete couldn't understand half of what was being said to him. But, he did get the idea that they were glad to see him. This dispelled any feelings foreboding he had been experiencing.

After the initial chaos of greeting things settled down and everyone was able to speak and be understood. The first question asked was what was he doing there? He answered that he was part of a negotiating team that was trying to get a deal done with a Japanese auto manufacturer. Then it was his turn to speak.

"Gentlemen, I am so sorry that I sent you on that mission. I should have known that if Dobbs was involved that there had to be something wrong with it. But, please believe me that if I had it to do over again you would never have gone." Pete said as his voice cracked.

"Pete.... We don't blame you. We blame that weasel Dobbs. He was the one who set us up, not you. You may have been our commander, but you were also our friend." Dick said.

"Since you have called me your friend, I am here to tell you that whatever you need I'll find a way to make it happen." Pete replied.

"Can you make my parents come back so I can say good bye?" Kelly said angrily.

"No Kelly, I can't. But believe me I wished I could. I know this makes you angry, but there is nothing I can do about it. If I could snap my fingers I would make all the hurt you're feeling go away.... But I can't. This is just something nobody can help you with, you're just going to have to learn how to go on and live your life the best you can." Pete replied, "By the way Kelly I want a private word with you when we're finished here." Kelly just shrugged and said OK.

The rest of the evening was filled with the camaraderie the team had enjoyed before their ill-fated mission. Pete sat back and just observed the men and tried to judge how much they had changed. The only one not taking as active role in the conversation was Kelly. He sat and kept pretty much to himself. He would answer questions that asked to him but as far as volunteering any direct comments into the conversation he was not forthcoming. Finally, about eleven o'clock Captain McDonald interrupted the party and said that they needed to get back so as not to wake up the rest of the patients. This brought boos and hisses from the team. They finally reluctantly agreed to return to the hospital.

"Jim.... Could I keep Kelly with me for a little while please." Pete asked. "Sure Colonel, who am I to say no to an officer who can make my life miserable." Jim replied with a smile. Soon the team left, and it was just Kelly and Pete sitting at the table. The waitress came around and Pete ordered them another round of drinks.

"Alright Kelly, I understand you wanted to talk to me so now is your chance.... Speak." Pete said bluntly.

"OK, here it is. My enlistment has been up for about two years and as you know my parents were killed in a car crash. But when they died they left me the ranch. Now my uncle has been looking after it since my parent's death, but when I spoke to him on the phone today he said he didn't want the ranch. Now my problem is, do I keep the ranch and just go home and work the land or do I sell it and try to stay in the army." Kelly explained. He met Pete's eyes with a steady stare that begged for advice.

Pete sat and looked at Kelly for a minute, then said, "Kelly, you know that I spent my entire life in the army. It treated me good. But, right now there is a reduction in force going on and they are putting out soldiers without at least ten years of service Because of that I don't think they'll let you stay in, but I have something I'd like to offer you. I'd like to offer you a position as a corporate investigator for Cleaver Chemical. Basically, you would stay at your ranch until we need you to investigate something or someone. We would pay you a retainer fee when you're not working. You'll have an office down the hall from me and I want you to feel free to come and go in your office as you see fit. How's that sound?" Pete asked hopefully.

Kelly sat and stared down at the tablecloth for a few moments then said, "Pete are you offering me this out of guilt or do you really think I can do the job? I mean I don't have any kind of experience in investigations, I wouldn't know where to start."

"Guilt? Kelly the only thing I'm guilt of is maybe not checking out Dobbs better than I did. But as far as you being able to do the job I have no doubt about it. Now do you want the job or not?" Pete replied gruffly.

"You're serious then, this isn't some softball you're tossing at me?" Kelly said.

"Hell no it ain't no softball. If you want the job, it's yours." Pete snorted. "What about the rest of the guys? Are you going to offer them jobs also?"

Kelly asked.

"No.... but they will be taken care of. I'm going to make sure of that." Pete replied.

"Pete there is just one thing I have to know, when you found out about us getting captured.... Did you really cry?" Kelly asked.

Pete sat for a long moment before he answered, "Yes Kelly I did. It was because I have a special feeling for you guys. You're like the younger brothers I never had. I could see greatness in each one of you, even Scuzzy Bill. Your fortitude during your captivity has proven me right. You looked out for each other as best you could given the situation. But make no mistake, if you screw up I'll either kick your ass or you'll kick mine. You got that?"

"That would be a fight to see." Kelly replied chuckling. Pete sat for a moment then began to chuckle also.

# EPILOGUE

*A note from the author*

Although this story is a work of fiction, like most stories it is based in truth. There are many veterans of Viet Nam, Afghanistan, and Iraq who carry the hidden scars of Post-traumatic stress disorder. This affliction can be cured by intense therapy and understanding by their families and friends.

Recently a study by the Veterans Administration concluded that one in ten veterans was suffering from post-traumatic disorder. Currently, because of the over-whelming numbers that are seeking help, the Veterans Healthcare System is not equipped to deal with so many clients. Some of the soldiers and sailors being referred to doctors outside the healthcare system. That is good except that most doctors are not fully educated in how to treat such an affliction because they normally don't see it.

I can speak to this malady because I have suffered from it for many years until I was fortunate enough to find a doctor who was able to recognize it for what it was. I had previously been diagnosed with everything from paranoia to schizophrenia to personality disorders (whatever that is). But it was until a doctor in Tucson, Arizona finally figured out what the problem was. He started forcing me to remember some of the things that had frightened me so bad. He gave me some medications that helped dispel the nightmares and level out my moods.

By the time I had found this doctor I had been through two marriages and was well on my way to becoming an alcoholic. But as I said this doctor was more worried about saving the patient then seeing how many patients he could push across his desk in a day.

So please remember that these men have been put through a meat grinder and survived. They deserve all the respect you can muster.

And to my fellow veterans who suffer from this most cruel of afflictions

May God bless you one and all

Thank you
Russ Stallings
*Author*

www.ingramcontent.com/pod-product-compliance
Ingram Content Group UK Ltd.
Pitfield, Milton Keynes, MK11 3LW, UK
UKHW022214230426
12048UKWH00016BA/842